An Unwanted Guest . . .

Clint and Sonnet had checked two large saloons before they came to the Golden Garter. They entered and went to the bar, ordered two beers.

"Don't look around," Clint said as the bartender set the beers down. "Just tell me if Dix Williams is in the place."

"He sure is."

"Where?" Sonnet asked.

"Behind you," the bartender said. "The girl with the green dress is in his lap, only she don't wanna be."

"He a friend of yours?" Clint asked.

"Hell, no," the man said. "He's been ridin' roughshod over this town since he got here. You'd be doin' us all a favor if you killed him."

Sonnet looked at Clint, who avoided his gaze.

"Okay," Clint said. "Thanks."

"Are you gonna?" the man asked.

"What?" Clint asked.

"Kill 'im?"

"No . . ." Clint said.

"But I am," Jack Sonnet said, and turned.

DON'T MISS THESE
ALL-ACTION WESTERN SERIES
FROM THE BERKLEY PUBLISHING GROUP

THE GUNSMITH by J. R. Roberts
Clint Adams was a legend among lawmen, outlaws, and ladies.
They called him . . . the Gunsmith.

LONGARM by Tabor Evans
The popular long-running series about Deputy U.S. Marshal
Custis Long—his life, his loves, his fight for justice.

SLOCUM by Jake Logan
Today's longest-running action Western. John Slocum rides a
deadly trail of hot blood and cold steel.

BUSHWHACKERS by B. J. Lanagan
An action-packed series by the creators of Longarm! The rous-
ing adventures of the most brutal gang of cutthroats ever
assembled—Quantrill's Raiders.

DIAMONDBACK by Guy Brewer
Dex Yancey is Diamondback, a Southern gentleman turned
con man when his brother cheats him out of the family fortune.
Ladies love him. Gamblers hate him. But nobody pulls one
over on Dex . . .

WILDGUN by Jack Hanson
The blazing adventures of mountain man Will Barlow—from
the creators of Longarm!

TEXAS TRACKER by Tom Calhoun
J.T. Law: the most relentless—and dangerous—manhunter in
all Texas. Where sheriffs and posses fail, he's the best man to
bring in the most vicious outlaws—for a price.

THE GUNSMITH

379

THE DEVIL'S COLLECTOR

J. R. ROBERTS

JOVE BOOKS, NEW YORK

THE BERKLEY PUBLISHING GROUP
Published by the Penguin Group
Penguin Group (USA) Inc.
375 Hudson Street, New York, New York 10014, USA

USA | Canada | UK | Ireland | Australia | New Zealand | India | South Africa | China

Penguin Books Ltd., Registered Offices: 80 Strand, London WC2R 0RL, England
For more information about the Penguin Group, visit penguin.com.

THE DEVIL'S COLLECTOR

A Jove Book / published by arrangement with the author

Jove Books are published by The Berkley Publishing Group.
JOVE® is a registered trademark of Penguin Group (USA) Inc.
The "J" design is a trademark of Penguin Group (USA) Inc.

For information, address: The Berkley Publishing Group,
a division of Penguin Group (USA) Inc.,
375 Hudson Street, New York, New York 10014.

ISBN: 978-0-515-15387-3

PUBLISHING HISTORY
Jove mass-market edition / July 2013

PRINTED IN THE UNITED STATES OF AMERICA

10   9   8   7   6   5   4   3   2   1

Cover illustration by Sergio Giovine.

ALWAYS LEARNING   **PEARSON**

ONE

DANEHILL, ARIZONA

Clint Adams was not usually on this side of the gunfight.

That is to say, on the sidelines, watching.

When he rode into Danehill, Arizona, he had no idea what he was getting into. He reined in his horse in front of the first saloon he came to. There were already a few horses there. He'd been thinking the last few miles of only one thing—a cold beer.

He entered the saloon, which at first looked like a small, sleepy place. There was only one table that had more than one man at it. Four cowboys were sitting together, and three were obviously subservient to one, a man with a flat-brimmed black hat and feral eyes.

"Help ya?" the bartender asked.

"I'd like to start with a cold beer," Clint said, "and then find someplace that cooks up a good steak."

"You can get both right here," the man told him.

"That right? Why don't we start with the beer, and if it's cold enough, I'll stay here for the steak."

"Comin' up," the bartender said.

He brought Clint a sweaty mug of cold beer with an impressive head. Clint took one sip and said, "Toss that steak on the stove."

"Take a seat," the man told him. "I'll bring it out."

At the table Del Colbert watched the man walk in and approach the bar.

"Anybody know that feller who just walked in?" he asked.

"Where?" Saul Tackett asked.

"At the bar, stupid," Colbert said.

The other three men all looked, then turned back to Colbert.

"Don't know 'im," Adam Kennedy said.

"Me neither," Cal Griffin said.

Tackett looked at Colbert and shook his head.

"Ah, what the hell," Colbert said. "Just some stranger gettin' a beer."

He went back to his own drink.

Jack Sonnet rode into town slowly, carefully. He scanned both sides of the street, as well as the rooftops. Satisfied nobody with a rifle had a bead on him, he directed his attention straight ahead.

His eyes were attracted to the horses tethered in front of the saloon. He reined in and studied the animals for a few moments, then dismounted and tied his own horse off next to the big black gelding, who turned his head to stare at him balefully.

Sonnet stepped up on to the boardwalk, took a look in the front window. He spotted the man he thought he was looking for, but he had to be sure.

He walked up to the batwing doors and went in.

* * *

As the batwings opened, Clint saw the young man enter. He looked too young to shave, but Clint noticed something about his eyes. They were alert, didn't miss a thing. The Colt tied down on his thigh also told him something. It was very well cared for.

Clint had a feeling things were going to get interesting. This boy was looking for somebody.

This time, when Colbert said, "Anybody know this kid?" he got a positive answer.

"Oh yeah," Kennedy said.

"Who is he?"

"Just some kid fancies himself a gunhand," Kennedy said.

"Why would he be here?" Colbert asked.

Kennedy shrugged.

"Would he be lookin' for you, Kennedy?" Colbert asked.

"Maybe," the man said.

"What did you do?"

"I mighta killed somebody," Kennedy said.

"Somebody?"

Kennedy shrugged again. "His older brother maybe."

"Shit," Colbert said. "When was that?"

"About three months ago, when I was in—"

"I don't care where you were," Colbert hissed. "Why didn't you tell me this?"

"You wouldn'ta let me come along if you knew," Kennedy said.

"You got that right!" Colbert said. "If this kid is here lookin' for you, Kennedy, you're on your own."

"Ah," Kennedy said, "I can take him . . ."

TWO

Clint expected the kid to walk to the bar. Instead, he walked directly to the table with the four men. They looked up at him curiously.

"You know any of these people?" Clint asked the bartender.

"Not a one," the man said, "including you."

Clint turned with his beer in his hand to watch . . .

"Can we help you?" Colbert asked.

"I'm lookin' for a man named Kennedy," the kid said. "Adam Kennedy."

"That's me," Kennedy said. He was across the table from the kid. "Who are you?"

"My name's Sonnet," the kid said, "Jack Sonnet."

"And what do you want with me?"

"You remember my brother?" Sonnet asked. "Carl Sonnet?"

"I remember."

"You killed him."

"I remember that, too," Kennedy said. "In a fair fight. He deserved it. Thought he was a fast gun. Well, he wasn't fast enough, was he?"

"No, he wasn't," Sonnet said, "but I am."

"Oh, you think so?" Kennedy asked with a loud belly laugh.

"I know so," Sonnet said. "No brag, just fact."

"So I suppose you want me to step outside?"

"Nope," Sonnet said, "right here'll do."

Clint knew what was coming. He could see it in Sonnet's face and demeanor that he meant to draw. The other man—Kennedy—started to get up, but then the other three did the same.

He couldn't just stand by.

"Hold it!" he snapped.

The four men turned and looked at him. Sonnet did not.

"What?" Colbert asked.

"What's your name?" Clint asked.

"Colbert."

"You're the leader here," Clint said. "At least, that's the way it looks to me."

"That's right. So?"

"So I think you and your other two boys should sit back down and keep your hands on the table."

"And why should we do that?"

"Because it sounds to me like this boy has a legitimate beef with your friend there. I think he should be allowed to settle it, man-to-man. Don't you?"

Sonnet still had not looked over at Clint. He was staring intently at the man called Kennedy.

"What's it to you?" Colbert said.

"Simple," Clint said. "I'll kill the first man who tries to interfere."

"Why?"

"Because he shouldn't have to face four men to get his satisfaction," Clint said. "One will do."

While Sonnet and Kennedy eyed each other, the other three men looked at Clint.

"You think you can take the three of us?" Colbert asked.

"I know I can," Clint said, then added, "No brag, just fact."

At that the kid sneaked a look at Clint, then gave him a nod.

"It's okay, Del," Kennedy said. "I can take him without help."

"You think so?" Colbert asked.

"Sure."

"All right, then," Colbert said, sitting back down. He looked at Clint. "But only 'cause you said so, Adam, not because he said so."

Kennedy stood up all the way and faced the kid.

"You called it, kid," he said. "The first move's yours."

Sonnet didn't say another word. He drew and fired. Kennedy never got a chance to put his hand on his gun. His body flew backward as if jerked by a chain. The kid was using a .44.

Colbert and the other two looked startled, looked at the kid, then looked at Clint.

Sonnet holstered his gun.

"Nobody move," Clint said to the men at the table.

"He killed our friend."

"In a fair fight."

"The kid's a gunny," Colbert said. "You saw him."

"Yeah, I saw him."

Clint could see how badly Colbert wanted to pull his gun.

"Okay, then go ahead," Clint said. "All of you. Throw down, but it'll be on the two of us, not just the kid."

"I ain't a kid," Sonnet said.

"All right," Clint said, "sorry. My mistake. The young man."

"He's a killer!" Colbert said.

"*He* was the killer," Sonnet said, pointing to the dead man. "I did the world a favor by killin' him."

The other three men stood up, but didn't make a move for their guns.

The batwings opened and a man with a badge on his chest and a gun in his hand entered.

"Everybody hold it!" he said.

"He did it!" Colbert yelled, pointing at Sonnet. "He killed Kennedy."

The sheriff looked at Sonnet.

"It was a fair fight," the young man said. "That man and the bartender were witnesses."

"Eddie?" the sheriff said to the bartender.

"That fella," Eddie said, indicating Sonnet, "came in and called that guy"—pointing to the dead man—"out. Those three"—pointing—"tried to back that one's play, but this one"—pointing at Clint—"stopped them. Then those two threw down. The kid outdrew him clean. The other fella never got a chance to touch his gun."

"So," the sheriff said, "six involved and one dead?"

"That's the way it looked to me," Eddie said.

"I wasn't involved," Clint said. "I just made sure it stayed a fair fight."

"And what's your name?" the sheriff asked.

Clint thought about lying. He wasn't going to walk away

from this once he gave the lawman his name. In the end, though, he told the truth.

"Clint Adams."

All the men in the room turned and looked at him. Colbert and his two companions suddenly drew their hands as far away from their guns as they could.

"Okay," the sheriff said, "Eddie, go around and collect all their guns."

"Sure, Sheriff."

The bartender went to the three men at the table and got their guns. Next he bent over and picked up the dead man's gun, and then confronted Sonnet, who handed his weapon over. Finally he walked over to Clint and stood in front of him, waiting.

"Here you go," Clint said, handing the man his gun. He could see the man release the breath he'd been holding.

"All right," the sheriff said, "everybody over to my office so we can sort this out. Eddie, get some men to carry the body over to the undertaker's."

"Sure, Sheriff."

The lawman waved his gun and said, "Let's go."

THREE

Sheriff Tom Booker did not put any of them in a cell.

There were only two chairs. The sheriff asked Sonnet to take one, and Clint the other.

"What's the Gunsmith doing in my town?" Booker asked.

"Looking for a cold beer and a steak," Clint said, "which is probably burnt by now."

"You can get another one," Booker said. He looked at the young man. "Your name is Sonnet?"

"That's right."

"That's a pretty famous name."

Sonnet shrugged.

"Are you part of that family?"

"Yes."

"See?" Colbert said. "See, I tol' you he was a gunman."

"You shut up," Booker said. "The bartender and Mr. Adams heard your friend confess that he killed this man's brother."

"In a fair fight!" Colbert protested.

"You mean the way you wanted it to happen here?" Clint asked. "You three were gonna draw down on this kid."

"I'm not a kid," Sonnet said.

Booker ignored him.

"We were gonna back our friend."

"Four against one?" the sheriff said. "If Mr. Adams hadn't stopped you, you'd all be in my jail right now."

Colbert frowned. The other two men just kept quiet. They were just happy they hadn't tried to draw on a Sonnet, and the Gunsmith, or they'd all be dead.

"All right," Booker said, sitting back in his chair, "you three can go."

"What about our guns?"

"You'll get them back when you leave town."

"We're gonna leave now."

"You'll leave in the mornin'," Booker said. "You'll get them back then. Now get out!"

"Are you givin' them their guns back?"

"Out!"

The three men slunk out of the office.

"Now you two," Booker said.

"I'm not leaving here without my gun, Sheriff," Clint said. "I'm a walking target without it."

"I understand that," Booker said. "But I don't need anyone else killed."

"I haven't killed anyone at all," Clint said.

"That's true."

"And I doubt Mr. Sonnet here has plans to kill anyone else."

"That's right," Sonnet said, "I don't."

Booker stared at them both for a few moments, then opened his drawer and took out their guns. He set them on the desk.

"I need you both to leave town," he said. "The sooner the better."

"Tomorrow morning?" Clint asked.

"Right now," Booker said. "You've still got a few hours of daylight."

"That suits me," Sonnet said. "I planned on leaving right after anyway."

"I have no problem with that either," Clint said, "although I'd like that steak."

"Then have your steak," Booker said, "and ride out right after."

"Okay," Clint said, "thanks, Sheriff."

They both picked their guns up off the desk and holstered them.

"Oh," the lawman said, "don't go back to the saloon for your steak. There's a café down the street called Victor's. Best steaks in town."

"Thanks again."

Clint and Sonnet left the office.

"I owe you," Sonnet said. "Let me buy you that steak. I could use one myself."

"That works for me," Clint said. "Let's go."

FOUR

They found the café the sheriff recommended to them, went inside, and got a table with no trouble, as it was too late for the townspeople to be eating lunch, and too early for supper.

After the waiter took their order and poured them some coffee, Clint said, "I knew your grandfather."

"Will?"

Clint nodded. "And your dad, but only some."

Sonnet nodded.

"They were both real fast," Clint said. "I think you're actually faster."

"Might be," Jack Sonnet said. "But I never would've said that to Grandpa. And I never would've wanted to test it out either."

"No, me neither," Clint said. "Even late in his life, he was like lightning."

"He sure was." A small smile was the first hint of emotion from the young man.

"Where you headed after this?"

"Wichita."

"What's in Kansas?"

Sonnet sipped his coffee and didn't answer.

"Oh," Clint said, "you're not finished hunting, are you?"

"No," Sonnet said. "It took more than that one man to kill my brother, Carl."

"How many?"

"Four."

"And this man, Kennedy?"

"He's the first I found."

"How many in Wichita?"

"One that I know of," Sonnet said. "I heard he settled there."

"When was your brother killed?"

"Three months ago."

"And it's taken you this long to find the first man?" Clint asked. "Not that I'm criticizing you now. No offense."

"None taken. I was laid up for a while."

"What happened?"

"I was bushwhacked," Jack said. "I was hurt bad, but survived. Carl didn't."

"Shot at the same time?"

Jack shook his head, then said, "Well, same time maybe, but different places."

"Sounds like it might've been planned?"

"That's what I'm thinkin'."

"By the same men?"

"No," Jack said, "happened about fifty miles apart. I was on my way to meet him in Monroe City, Colorado. I was laid up a month. When I got to Monroe City, I heard he'd been shot in the street by five men."

"And you got their names?"

Sonnet nodded. "Some of 'em. I know where to get the rest."

"What about those three who were with Kennedy?" Clint asked. "Any of them?"

They had heard all the men's names in the sheriff's office.

"No," Sonnet said. "I never heard of any of them. He was just ridin' with them now, I guess."

"Well," Clint said, "they might not be done with you yet."

"That'd be too bad for them," Sonnet said.

The waiter came and set their steaks down. They were both starving, so they tucked in and left the rest of the talk for later.

Then, over dessert, Clint asked, "Do you have anybody you can ask to back your play?"

"No," Sonnet said. "I'll do this myself."

"What if you get bushwhacked again?"

"I'm gonna try not to."

"You can't have eyes in back of your head."

"My grandpa did."

"Yeah, he did." Clint laughed.

"I'll bet you do, too."

Clint didn't answer. Even though he was good at watching his own back, he did have people he could ask for help if he needed it. And in spite of that, he figured that was the way he was eventually going to leave this world, shot in the back, like Hickok.

"What about me?" he asked.

"What about you?"

"I could watch your back."

"I ain't askin'."

"I know that," Clint said. "I'm offering."

"Why?"

"I told you," Clint said, "I knew your grandpa. He was a hell of a man. I can't just stand by and watch his grandson get gunned down."

"Well," Sonnet said, "you did save my bacon in the saloon."

"You might have been able to take them."

"I might've," Sonnet agreed.

"What do you say?"

Sonnet thought a moment.

"Am I gonna have to keep buyin' the steaks?"

"No," Clint said. "We'll split the cost of the meals, and supplies."

"Well then," Sonnet said, "I don't see any reason why not."

"I don't either."

Sonnet put his right hand out.

"I thank you, Clint," he said, "for what you did, and for what you're offerin' now."

"You're welcome." They shook hands.

"One thing, though."

"What's that?"

"When we find the men we're looking for, they're mine," Sonnet said.

"Agreed," Clint said. "I'm just there to watch your back, and keep things fair."

"All right, then," Sonnet said. He looked around for the waiter. "Let's settle up and get moving."

FIVE

Dixon Williams stepped from the general store and took a deep breath. The Wichita streets were busy, with foot traffic as well as wagons and buckboards going by. Anybody not watching where they were going when they crossed the street was likely to get run over. Kids playing in the streets yelled at each other and dodged the wheels, enjoying the danger. Dix knew if their mothers could see them, they'd be in a lot more danger.

Dix had arrived in Wichita only a couple of months ago, but he'd arrived with a wallet full of cash. Tired of making his living from stealing and killing, and the life he'd been leading, he bought himself a piece of the general store, and now he was a businessman. On top of that, he had a woman in town who—he hoped—felt the same way about him that he felt about her.

In quite a reversal of fortunes, life could not have gotten any better for Dix Williams.

Clint Adams and Jack Sonnet rode into Wichita in the afternoon. They'd been riding a long time and were bone tired.

The only good thing about spending that much time on the trail was that they had gotten to know each other a lot better.

Sonnet enjoyed listening to the stories Clint had to tell about knowing not only his grandfather, but also the likes of Bat Masterson, Wyatt Earp, Buffalo Bill Cody, and Luke Short.

Sonnet, Clint learned, was twenty-four, although he looked younger. That was something that bothered the younger man, who did not like being called "kid." Clint could understand that. He most assuredly was not a kid. Not anymore.

Killing a man—or men—made someone grow up awfully fast.

"Hotel," Clint said, using his chin to point.

"Sheriff's office," Sonnet said.

"Let's find the livery, get the horses settled," Clint said. "After that we can get a room, and then a hot meal."

"That all sounds good to me," Sonnet said.

At the livery Clint and Sonnet decided to unsaddle their own horses, but they allowed the livery owner to rub them down and feed them.

They left the stable with their saddlebags and rifles, stopped at the first saloon they came to, The Royal Rose.

"Two beers," Clint said at the bar.

They looked around, found the place about half full of sleepy-looking men.

"See anybody matching the description?" Clint asked.

"No," Sonnet said, "but we've got a name. All we gotta do is ask around."

"Guess that depends."

"On what?"

"On whether your man is passing through, or he settled here."

"Why would a killer settle down here?"

"Maybe he's tired of killing," Clint said. "Everybody settles down eventually."

"Are you ever gonna settle down?"

"Well," Clint said, "that's different. I don't think I'll ever settle down."

"Really? Why not? Everybody's always tellin' me to get married and have a family."

"Well, not me," Clint said. "Not with my reputation. If I settled down in one place, too many wannabe gunfighters would know just where to find me."

"I guess that's the price you have to pay for a reputation," Sonnet said. "Happened to my pa, and my grandpa."

"Well, you've still got time to keep it from happening to you."

"How do you mean?"

"Give this thing up," Clint said. "Get on with your life."

"Is that what you'd do?"

"Now? No," Clint said, "but at your age, maybe."

"Well, I can't," Sonnet said. "I have to get this done, Clint."

"Okay, then," Clint said. He turned and waved the bartender over.

"Yes, sir?"

"You know where we can find a man named Dixon Williams?"

"Dix Williams?" the bartender said. "Sure. He's part owner of the general store, just down the street."

Sonnet frowned.

"He's a merchant?"

"Sure is."

Sonnet looked at Clint.

"That can't be the right man."

Clint looked at the bartender.

"How long has he owned the general store?"

"Well, I figure he came to town a couple of months ago, bought him a piece of the place. Don't know what he was doing before that."

"I do," Sonnet said. He slammed his mug down on the bar, turned, and left.

"Thanks," Clint said. He put his mug down, paid the man, and hurried after Sonnet.

"Jack!"

Clint caught up to him, grabbed his arm.

"What?"

"Don't go off half-cocked."

"I just wanna make sure it's the right man," Sonnet said.

"Sounds like it could be."

"What the hell is he doing bein' a store owner?" the younger man asked.

"Maybe he's trying to change his life," Clint said.

"Well, it's too late for that," Sonnet said.

"We've got to be careful, Jack," Clint said. "If he's a town merchant now, you can't just gun him down."

"I'll give him a chance," Sonnet said. "Same chance him and his partners gave my brother."

"Maybe," Clint said, "we should just go into the store and you should let me do the talking for now."

"Well, all right," Sonnet said, "but I ain't gonna wait for long, Clint. I've got to get this done and move on to the next one."

"And where is that?"

"I don't know yet," Sonnet said. "I'm waitin' for a telegram."

Sonnet was getting information from somebody about

where these men he was hunting were, but Clint didn't know who was feeding him the info. At some point, he was going to have to ask.

"All right," Clint said. "Let's go and see what's going on at the general store."

SIX

They entered the general store, which was actually called Grenke's Emporium. The inside was very spacious, and they seemed to have everything a person could need, from men and women's clothes to staples to weapons and ammunition.

There was an older man with gray hair, wearing a white body-length apron, stocking shelves in the back, and an attractive girl in her twenties behind the counter, waiting on customers.

Clint stepped up to the counter, with Sonnet close behind. The girl finished waiting on a middle-aged woman, who turned to leave then stopped and stared when she saw Clint standing there.

"Oh!"

"Sorry to startle you, ma'am," Clint said.

"Hmph," the woman said, and went around him.

"Can I help you, sir?" the girl asked with a bright smile. She sneaked a look past him at Sonnet.

"Yes, ma'am," Clint said, "my friend and I are looking for Dixon Williams."

"Dix?" she asked. "You just missed him."

"That's too bad," Clint said. "Can you tell us where he went?"

"I'm not sure," she said.

"I understand he owns this store?"

"I own this store," the older man said firmly.

"Dix bought a piece of the business from my father when he came to town a few months ago," the girl explained.

"Huh," the older man said. "Sarah, go take care of the women's clothes."

"There's nothin' wrong with the women's clothes, Pa."

"Move'em around," the man growled.

She looked down, then said to Clint, "Excuse me," and slid from behind the counter.

"My name's Ed Grenke. You friends of his?" the man asked. "Dixon Williams?"

"I wouldn't say that," Clint replied.

"Well, he forced me to sell him a piece of my business cheap."

"Forced how?"

"How d'ya think?" the man asked. "He threatened me."

"You go to the sheriff?"

"The man is useless," Grenke said. "If you're here for Dix Williams, good luck to you."

"Do you know where he is, Mr. Grenke?" Sonnet asked.

"If I was you, I'd look in a saloon," Grenke said. "One of the bigger ones."

"Thank you," Clint said.

They started to leave, then Clint stopped and turned back.

"Does he have any friends in town?" he asked.

"Not a one."

"Thanks."

"Do us all a favor," Grenke said as they went out the door. "Kill 'im."

As they stepped out, Sonnet looked at Clint.

"Don't say it."

"I don't have to," Sonnet said. "Come on, let's find him and get this over with."

Williams lifted the shot glass to his mouth, drained it, then poured himself a fresh drink. The saloon girl sitting in his lap wriggled in his grasp.

"Sit still, damn it!" he snapped.

"I gotta go to work, Dix," she complained.

"You are workin', darlin'," he told her.

She looked toward the bartender for help, but he averted his eyes. Nobody wanted to go against Dix Williams's gun.

The rest of the patrons in the Golden Garter Saloon paid attention to their own drinking. They ignored Dix Williams as long as he ignored them.

Williams really liked this town. He had a new business, plenty of money, plenty of women in town—including the daughter of his "partner"—and he had the run of it all.

His life couldn't get any better.

Clint and Sonnet had checked two large saloons before they came to the Golden Garter. They entered and went to the bar, ordered two beers.

"Don't look around," Clint said as the bartender set the beers down. "Just tell me if Dix Williams is in the place."

"He sure is."

"Where?" Sonnet asked.

"Behind you," the bartender said. "The girl with the green dress is in his lap, only she don't wanna be."

"He a friend of yours?" Clint asked.

"Hell, no," the man said. "He's been ridin' roughshod over this town since he got here. You'd be doin' us all a favor if you killed him."

Sonnet looked at Clint, who avoided his gaze.

"Okay," Clint said. "Thanks."

"Are you gonna?" the man asked.

"What?" Clint asked.

"Kill 'im?"

"No . . ." Clint said.

"But I am," Jack Sonnet said, and turned.

SEVEN

"Dix Williams!"

The man looked up at the sound of his name, craned his neck to look around the girl.

"You talkin' to me, kid?" he asked.

"I am."

"I'm a little busy at the moment."

Sonnet walked forward, grabbed the girl's arm, and pulled her from Williams's grasp.

"Go away," he told her.

"Thank you," she said and rushed over to the bar.

"You lookin' for trouble, boy?" Williams demanded. He was just drunk enough to be loud and blustery.

"I'm lookin' for you, Dix," Sonnet said.

"Do I know you?"

"Sort of."

"Whataya mean, sort of?"

"You knew my brother."

"I did?" Williams asked. "How well?"

"Well enough to kill him."

Williams did not look surprised that Sonnet was the brother of a man he'd killed.

"You know," he said proudly, stretching his legs out, "I know a lot of dead brothers."

"Well, you're not gonna know any more after today."

"That's big talk for a kid who's wet behind the ears," William said. "Is your friend backin' your play?"

Clint raised his hands and said, "I'm out of it."

"Stand up," Sonnet said.

"This'll do me just fine," Williams said, his legs still stretched out ahead of him.

"Fine," Sonnet said. He drew and fired.

With just a quick tremor of his extended legs, Dix Williams died.

The place grew quiet, and then the girl in the green dress said, "Oh, thank God."

Before long, men were slapping Sonnet on the back and pumping his hand.

This was not exactly the reaction Clint wanted Sonnet to experience after killing a man.

He turned around and said to the bartender, "Two more beers."

"Yes, *sir*," the bartender said. "On the house!"

EIGHT

When the sheriff arrived, he didn't take them to his office. He took them to the mayor's office.

His name was Andy Green, and Clint could see what Ed Grenke meant when he said the man was useless. He was completely unimpressive as physical specimens go, and apparently devoid of good sense. He let them keep their guns as he escorted them to the mayor's office.

"Gentlemen," the mayor said as they entered, "please, have a seat."

They both sat in front of his desk.

"That's all, Andy."

"But sir—"

"Go."

He went.

The mayor was a tall, slender man in his fifties, wearing a three-piece suit. He sat back in his chair and regarded them.

"I need your names."

"Clint Adams."

"Jack Sonnet."

"I'm Mayor Leon Polk. Which one of you killed Dix Williams?"

"I did," Sonnet said.

"You're kind of young."

Sonnet just stared at the man.

"And what did you do?" the mayor asked Clint.

"I just watched."

"And backed him up."

"In case Williams had some friends."

"Not much danger in that," the mayor said. "I'm quite glad you killed him. We've been looking for a way to get him out of town."

"You're welcome."

"I know who you are, Mr. Adams," Polk said. "I was wondering if you'd entertain taking the position of town marshal?"

"No," Clint said.

"How about you, son?"

"You want me to be marshal?"

"Why not?"

"I have things to do."

"More men to kill?" Polk asked.

Again, he asked a question Jack Sonnet was not going to answer.

"All right, well," Mayor Polk said, "in that case I'll need you both to leave town before you kill someone else."

"That was our plan, Mayor," Clint said.

"Good," Polk said, "then we're on the same page."

"Definitely," Clint said.

"Then good day, gentlemen," Polk said. "And again, my thanks."

*   *   *

Outside on the street, Jack Sonnet asked, "Where to now?"

"A hotel," Clint said.

"I thought you told the mayor we were leavin' town," Sonnet said.

"We are," Clint said, "in the morning. I want the horses to have some rest and—oh, by the way—us, too. And since Dix Williams had no friends in town, I don't think we have to worry about reprisals."

"What about the sheriff?"

"Now, I really don't think we have anything to worry about from him, do you?"

"No," Sonnet said, "I suppose not."

"Besides," Clint said, "do you even know where we're going after this?"

"Not yet. I need to send a telegram."

"Okay, then," Clint said, "we'll get a room, something to eat, and then you send your telegram. Tomorrow we'll get going again."

NINE

"Coffee," the naked Carlotta Carlyle asked, "or me first?"

"You," Cole Damon said.

He reached out, grabbed her hands, and pulled her down on top of him. Her big breasts were solid cushions between them. They almost smothered him. He extricated his face from between them and chewed avidly on her large nipples.

Damon had been in Deline for a few weeks. He had gone to Carlotta's whorehouse the very first day and—after eyeing the girls in the sitting room—had decided on the madam herself. She was a few years older than he was, but that didn't matter much to him. She was also the richest woman in town.

She slithered down between his legs, fondled his thick cock until it was standing long and straight, and then took it into her expert mouth.

Damon thought this was the only way to wake up.

"Cole Damon," Sonnet told Clint as he handed a cup of coffee across the campfire.

He poured himself a cup and hunkered down so that they were on the same level.

"Damon," Clint said. "I never heard of him."

"What about Deline, Missouri?"

Clint shook his head.

"Never heard if that either."

Sonnet nodded and sipped his coffee.

"Do you mind if I ask you a few questions?" Clint asked.

"Sure, go ahead."

"Where have you been getting your information?"

Sonnet drank his coffee.

"I mean, I know through telegrams," Clint said, "but telegrams from where? And who?"

"I can't say."

"Won't, or can't?"

"No," Sonnet said, "I'd tell you if I could. I really can't, because I don't know who the telegrams come from."

"Now, wait," Clint said. "You're killing men based on information you're receiving from . . . you don't know who?"

"But he seems to know who they are, and where they are."

"But what if he's wrong?"

"He hasn't been," Sonnet said. "So far neither of them denied killing my brother."

"If they even remembered," Clint said.

"They remembered," Sonnet said. "I wouldn't pull the trigger if I didn't think they remembered."

"I'd like to believe that."

"Clint," Sonnet said, "I'm not just killing to kill. There's a reason."

"There seems to be a reason for somebody," Clint agreed.

"I think we should get mounted up," Sonnet said. "We can make Deline today."

"Sure," Clint said, "your call, Jack."

"I'll douse the fire," Sonnet said, standing up and dumping the remnants of his coffee into the already dying flames.

"And I'll saddle the horses," Clint said.

He walked over to where the horses were picketed, hoping that maybe he had given the younger man something to think about.

TEN

They rode into Deline later that night.

At the livery Clint said, "This time I want a steak, some pie and coffee, a beer, and then a room."

"You askin' or tellin'?" Sonnet asked.

"I'm asking," Clint said. "This is all your call, Jack."

"Well, it sounds good to me," Sonnet said. "Let's do it."

Clint was starting to get bored with it.

If all went according to plan, they would get to a town, take care of the horses, get a beer, maybe a meal, then Sonnet would find his target and kill him. Then move on to the next town.

Clint was starting to think a lot about who Sonnet was getting his information from. Could there be somebody out there with a kill list? Somebody who was using Sonnet to get the list cleared? And what if it had nothing to do with who killed his brother? How would the kid feel then?

Well, maybe he wasn't bored. Maybe he was worried

about what all this killing, all this vengeance, would do to Jack Sonnet. Could be he thought he owed it to the boy's father and grandpa to save the boy from this life.

"Why are you so quiet?" Sonnet asked, pushing his plate away.

"Just thinking."

"About what?"

"About you," Clint said.

"Don't tell me you're gonna start tryin' to talk me out of this now."

"Maybe," Clint said. "How many more you got, Jack?"

"Three."

"You know their names?"

"No," Sonnet said, "just this next one, Cole Damon."

"What do you say we ask a few more questions this time, Jack?"

"Like what? Why?"

"Like maybe we can find out if Damon really did know your brother."

Sonnet squinted.

"What are you saying?" Sonnet demanded. "You think somebody's feeding me the wrong names? Making me kill the wrong people?"

"Could be."

"Why would somebody want to do that?"

Clint shrugged.

"Then why are you thinking that?"

"You're wondering why I would think somebody might steer you wrong," Clint said. "Maybe I'm wondering why somebody would steer you right."

"To be helpful."

"People aren't helpful for no reason, Jack."

"Then why are you being helpful?"

"Believe me, I always have reasons for what I do," Clint assured him.

"Because of my pa and grandpa?"

"Yes."

"You owe it to them?"

"In a way."

"Well, maybe whoever's been sending me the telegrams owes it to them, too."

"Who do you think it is?" Clint asked. "Some old friend of your father or grandfather's?"

"You'd know who their friends were more than I would," Sonnet said.

"When did you first start getting them?"

"Soon after my brother was killed," Sonnet said. "I was trying to find the men who killed him on my own, with no luck. Then the first telegram caught up with me."

"So how do they know where you are, to send the telegrams?"

"I don't know."

Clint looked around. The only way someone could know where the kid was at all times was if they had someone following him, watching him. He looked around the small café they were in. There were a few other tables taken, but nobody seemed to be paying them any special attention.

"So you get these telegrams with the information, and you never questioned how or why?"

"No."

"Why not?"

Sonnet hesitated, then said, "I don't know."

"I do."

"Then share it with me," Sonnet said.

"You need the information," Clint said. "You needed it so bad that when it came, you jumped at it."

"The first two men I killed also killed my brother," Sonnet said. "I'm satisfied of that."

"It doesn't worry you that somebody might be using you?"

"No," Sonnet said. "Not as long as I get what I want." He pushed his chair back.

"Hey," Clint said, "we've still got to have pie, and then get a room."

"You have some pie," Sonnet said. "I'll get my own room and see you later."

"Yeah, but—" Clint started as Sonnet went out the door. "Which hotel?"

Clint called the waiter over and ordered peach pie.

ELEVEN

After his pie, Clint left the café and found the sheriff's office. He was sure Jack Sonnet was walking the streets and checking saloons for Cole Damon. He figured maybe he could go about it a different way. He figured if he got to Damon first, maybe he could find the answers to some of his questions.

The office was old and small. A lot like the town. Clint figured within ten years most of the people would have moved on. Certainly this sheriff would no longer be in office. It looked as if he was already on his last legs. He was seventy if he was a day, wearing overalls that were at least that old.

"Sheriff?"

The man looked up from his desk, eyed Clint from beneath two bushy white eyebrows. His head had more liver spots than hairs.

"I used to be, sonny," he said. "What are you doin' in this godforsaken town?"

"I'm looking for a man named Cole Damon. Ever heard of him?"

"I know everybody in this town," the man said. "I know when they ride in, and when they leave."

"That a fact?"

"You don't believe me?" The man laughed. "Yeah, I know I don't look like much. There was a time, though, when I was a lot of man."

"I can believe that."

"Well, I know what you had to eat at the café," the lawman said. "I know your friend left and you had peach pie for dessert."

"Then I guess you know where my friend is?"

"He hit a couple of the saloons," the sheriff said. "Still in one, I bet."

"Well, he's also looking for Cole Damon," Clint said. "I'd like to find him first."

"Which one of you wants to kill 'im?"

"Not me."

"Your friend?"

"He's got information that says Damon killed his brother."

"And you?" the sheriff asked. "Why do you want to find him?"

"I want to ask him if he did it or not."

"So you'll give him a chance to talk and your friend won't?"

"That's about the size of it."

"Well," the sheriff said, "if your friend hasn't already found him in one of the saloons, you'll find him over at Carlotta's."

"Carlotta's?"

"Cathouse."

"Okay, thanks."

"Hey?"

Clint stopped at the door.

"What's your name?"

"Clint Adams."

"For real?" The old man's eyes brightened.

"Yes, for real."

"Well, sonofagun," the man said. "My name's Jeremiah M. Atticus. I'm seventy years old, and you're the first famous person I ever met in my life. You'll probably be the last."

"Let's hope not, Sheriff," Clint said.

"Look, Mr. Adams," Atticus said, "you do what you gotta do in my town, and I'll be right here if you need me. Okay?"

"Okay, Sheriff."

"And if you want a decent steak, go to Molly's up the street."

"Sure thing. Thanks."

TWELVE

When Clint reached the whorehouse, he found a falling-down two-story wood-frame house that had actually seen some repairs. Probably just enough to make sure it remained standing.

He mounted the steps and knocked on the door. A pretty girl in a see-through nightie opened it. He could see her belly button, and her brown nipples. She had big blue eyes, a cute nose, and a cupid's bow mouth. He wondered if she was even fifteen.

"You lookin' for love, mister?"

"If I was, I wouldn't be here, darlin'," he said. "I'm looking for a man named Cole Damon. Is he here?"

"I think so," she said. "If he is, he's with Miss Carlotta."

"Well, could I come in and maybe you could find out for me?"

"Sure," she said. "Come on in."

He entered, looked to the right into a parlor filled with girls. Seemed like a lot of whores for this town.

"We serve the whole county," she said, as if reading his mind.

"I'm sure you do. What's your name?"

"Lila. What's yours?" she asked. "Miss Carlotta is gonna ask me."

"My name is Clint Adams."

"I'll check with Miss Carlotta."

Just moments before the girl knocked on Carlotta's door, Cole Damon had her legs spread wide and was driving his stiff penis in and out of her. She was grunting and moaning, but as a pro, she did not ever scream or yell out loud. Damon, however, let go with a loud growl as he exploded into her, a sound the girl heard while she was walking down the hall to the room. That was how she knew they were done when she knocked on the door.

"What?" Carlotta yelled as Damon dismounted.

"Miss Carlotta, there's a fella here lookin for Mr. Damon."

Carlotta looked at Damon.

"Is he a lawman?" Damon called out.

"No, sir."

"Who is it?" Carlotta asked.

"He says his name is Clint Adams."

Damon rushed to the door, still naked, and swung it open. His penis was still semihard and immediately drew Lila's eyes.

"Who?"

"Clint Adams."

"The Gunsmith?"

The girl shrugged, still staring at Damon's dick.

Damon turned and looked at Carlotta.

"Now what the hell's he want?" he asked.

"I don't know."

"Well," Damon said, turning to face her, "why don't you go out there and find out?"

Now that he turned around, Lila was staring at his naked ass.

Carlotta leaned over so she could see past Damon to Lila.

"Tell him I'll be right there."

"Yes, ma'am."

She didn't leave, though. She was still staring at Damon's body. She was used to seeing fat, old men come through the whorehouse. Not men who looked good, like Cole Damon.

"Lila!"

Startled, the girl turned and ran down the hall.

"She'll be right out," Lila told Clint. "Do you wanna wait in the parlor?"

"No, that's okay," Clint said. "I'll wait right here."

"Yes, sir."

Lila left him there and went into the parlor herself. Moments later a buxom blonde in her forties, carrying about thirty pounds too much weight, all of it in her breasts, came from a downstairs hall. She was out of breath, and her hair was tousled.

"You're Adams?" she asked.

"That's right," he said. "Miss Carlotta?"

"Lila says your name is Clint Adams," Carlotta said. "You're the Gunsmith, right?"

"That's right."

"And you're lookin' for Cole Damon?"

"Yes."

"What for?"

"To try to keep him alive."

THIRTEEN

Carlotta walked Clint down the hall to her room.

"Just let me talk to him first," she said.

"Sure," Clint said, "but tell him not to go out the window. There's no need."

"I'll tell him."

She opened the door and went inside. In a second, he heard raised voices. That went on for a few minutes, and then the door opened and Carlotta looked out.

"You can come in, Mr. Adams."

He entered, found himself immediately covered by Cole Damon's gun. The man was wearing a pair of jeans, and nothing else.

"There's no need for that," he tried to assure him.

"Just put yer hands up," Damon said.

Clint obeyed.

"Now why're you lookin' for me? I never did nothin' to you."

"That's true," Clint said. "I'm just trying to help you."

"Why?"

"I don't want to see you get killed."

"And who wants to kill me?"

"First," Clint said, "let me ask you if you knew a man named Carl Sonnet."

"Carl Sonnet?" Damon thought for a moment then replied, "I don't think so."

"Well," Clint said, "somebody thinks you did. In fact, he thinks you're one of the men who killed Carl Sonnet."

"Where'd this happen? When?"

"A few months ago," Clint said. "In Texas."

"I ain't been to Texas in years."

"Is that true?"

"It is."

"Can you prove it?"

"Do I have to?"

"Did you ever know men named Dell Colbert or Dix Williams?"

"Never."

Clint frowned.

"Why you askin' me all these questions? What's this you told Carlotta about me gettin' killed?"

"Carl Sonnet's kid brother, Jack, is searching the country for the men who killed his brother. When he finds them, he kills them."

"Murder?"

"Fair and square," Clint said. He outdraws them, clean."

"Ain't no kid gonna outdraw me," Damon said. "Unless you back his play."

"I'm actually riding with him, just to keep him from getting backshot."

"So you're helpin' him?"

"I have been," Clint said, "but I don't want to find that he's been killing innocent men. So I ask you again, did you kill Carl Sonnet?"

"I didn't."

"I think you're going to have to prove it, Mr. Damon," Clint said.

"Oh yeah? Why don't I just kill this kid when he comes for me?"

"Well, I wouldn't be able to let you do that."

"And what if I kill you now?"

"You didn't take my gun," Clint said, "and you know who I am. If you were going to kill me, you should have done it by now. I can still draw and kill you, even if you shoot me. Want to try?"

"No!" Carlotta said. "No shootin' in my place!"

"Then put it down, Damon," Clint said. "And let's talk. Convince me that you're innocent."

Damon lowered his gun, but he said, "Why should I be worried about this kid?"

"His name's Sonnet," Clint said. "That mean anything to you?"

"No," he said, then thought a moment. "Wait. Yes. You mean . . . those Sonnets?"

Clint nodded. "Those Sonnets. Carl wasn't good with a gun, but I've seen Jack kill two men now. You wouldn't stand a chance."

"Cole," Carlotta said. "Talk to him. Let him help you."

Damon licked his lips.

"Okay," he said, "okay. Lemme get dressed."

"Come with me," Carlotta said to Clint. "I got another room where you two can talk and have a drink."

"Okay," Clint said. Then to Damon, he warned, "But don't take too long."

"I'll be there."

Carlotta opened the door again and said, "This way, Mr. Gunsmith."

FOURTEEN

Carlotta took Clint to a room that looked like it was used to eat in, or play cards. There were several tables with chairs stacked on them.

A black man took down two of the chairs and set them on the floor.

"Isaac," Carlotta said, "please get a bottle of whiskey and three glasses."

"Yes, ma'am."

"Three glasses?" Clint asked.

"Well," she said, "I'm not the kind of hostess who lets her guests drink alone."

"I see."

"Um, have you talked to the sheriff about this?" she asked.

"Sheriff Atticus?" he said. "Yes, I stopped to see him first. Why?"

"I was just wonderin'."

At that moment Cole Damon came walking in, fully

dressed, his gun belt strapped on. Behind him came the black man with the whiskey bottle and three glasses. He set the glasses down, filled them, put the bottle on the table, and left the room.

Carlotta sat at the table and picked up one of the glasses. Both Clint and Damon looked at her.

"What?" she asked. "It's my house. Go ahead and have your talk."

Damon sat and grabbed a glass.

"What's this all about?" he asked Clint.

"Like I said," Clint answered, "I rode in with Jack Sonnet, who is convinced you're one of the men who killed his brother. You say you're not."

"I ain't killed no fella named Sonnet," Damon said.

"Okay, so we've got to convince Jack Sonnet of that."

"You convince him," Damon said. "He's your friend. If he comes after me, I'll kill 'im."

"You wouldn't stand a chance."

"You ain't seen me handle a gun."

"It doesn't matter," Clint said. "I have seen him use one, and I'm telling you, I wouldn't want to have to go up against him."

That seemed to surprise Damon, but he puffed out his chest and said, "Yeah, well, maybe you're just gettin' old."

"And maybe I want you to get older," Clint said. He looked at Carlotta. "Okay, now you talk to him."

"Cole—" she said, but he cut her off.

"Just be quiet, Carlotta!" he said. "I ain't afraid of no kid with a gun. You tell 'im that, Adams. You tell him not to come for me."

Clint stepped sway from the table. He hadn't touched the drink that had been poured for him.

"I'll tell him, Damon," Clint said, "but that doesn't mean

I'll be able to stop him. Look, all you've got to do is talk to the kid. Convince him you didn't kill his brother."

"I ain't gotta prove I didn't do it," Damon said. "He's gotta prove I did."

"That's just it," Clint said. "He doesn't have to prove it."

"Huh?"

"I'm not telling you he wants to take you to court," Clint said. "I'm saying he wants to kill you. He's satisfied you're one of the men who did it."

Damon thought that over, had himself another drink for courage, then told Clint, "You get outta here. You tell him what I said. He comes near me, I'll kill 'im."

"Isaac will show you out, Mr. Adams," Carlotta said. The black man appeared at the door. "Thank you."

"You're welcome, ma'am," Clint said.

After Clint left, Carlotta turned her attention to Damon.

"What are you tryin' to do?"

"I didn't do nothin' wrong," he insisted.

"That man came here to try and help you."

"Like hell he did," Damon said. "He's just scoutin' me out fer his friend."

"Cole," she said, "you have a chance to talk about this without it turnin' into a shootin'."

"Like hell."

"Cole—"

"If that kid comes for me, I'm gonna kill 'im," Cole Damon said, pouring himself another drink. "That's all there is to it."

"There's nothin' I can say to change your mind?" she asked.

"Nothin'."

She poured herself a drink.

"Then you're a damn fool!"

FIFTEEN

Clint didn't know where to find Jack Sonnet. All he knew was that Sonnet had not yet found Cole Damon.

He decided to get himself a room at the hotel closest to the last place he'd seen Sonnet, the café. Turned out there were only two hotels in town anyway, so it didn't matter.

He went to both hotels to see if Sonnet had checked in yet. He had not. So he picked one and got himself a room. He went upstairs, sat on the thin mattress for a moment, then walked to the window and stared out at the street. There didn't seem to be any way he could keep Cole Damon from waiting for Sonnet. What he was going to have to do was find the kid and try to convince him that Damon was innocent. He knew Jack Sonnet would never be able to forgive himself if he killed an innocent man.

At least, he hoped that was something he knew about the young man.

He walked to the door of his room and went out.

* * *

Clint found Sonnet in the second saloon he checked. While the town only had two hotels, it had five saloons.

Sonnet was standing at the bar with a beer in front of him. Clint stood next to him.

"You get a room?" Clint asked.

"Nope."

"I did. I'll take you over there so you can get one."

"Sure."

"What have you been doing?"

"Lookin'."

"You find him?"

"Not yet."

The bartender came over. "Somethin'?"

"A beer."

"Comin' up."

Clint realized Sonnet was looking at him.

"Oh, yeah, well," Clint said, "I did. I found him."

Sonnet turned to face him.

"Where is he?"

"First we have to talk."

"Why?"

The bartender brought over a cold beer. Clint picked it up and said, "Let's go sit down."

The place was practically empty, so they had their pick of tables.

"Come on," Clint said. "This won't take long."

Clint walked to a table, and Sonnet followed.

"What are you tryin' to pull?"

"I talked to the man," Clint said. "He says he's innocent."

"That's why I don't talk to them first," Sonnet said. "Not for long anyway."

"You did talk to the other two, and neither of them claimed they were innocent," Clint said. "But this one does."

"Clint—"

"Just listen for a second," Clint said. "What if he's telling the truth?"

"He's not."

"How do you know?"

"I know."

"No, Jack," Clint said, "you don't know, you've been told."

"Clint," Sonnet said, "where is he? You know I'll find him."

"Talk to him first, Jack."

Sonnet just stared at him.

"All right," Clint said wearily, "I'll take you to him."

Clint felt he had to take Sonnet to Cole Damon; otherwise the young man would find him on his own. And he might find him in the midst of a bunch of innocent bystanders.

"The whorehouse?" Sonnet said as they stopped in front of the building. "That's where he is?"

"That's where he is."

"Stay out of the way, Clint," Sonnet said.

"You can't go in there, Jack."

"Why not?"

"There are a lot of innocent people in there."

"I'm not going to accidentally hit a bystander," Sonnet said.

"Maybe you're not," Clint said, "but he might."

Sonnet studied Clint for a few moments, then said, "Yeah, okay."

He turned to face the building.

"Cole Damon!" he yelled. "Cole Damon, I'm calling you out!"

SIXTEEN

Inside, Carlotta looked at Damon.

"See?" Damon said. "Adams brought him." He stood up.

"Cole, go out the back," she said. "I'll keep them busy."

"I ain't runnin' from no kid," Damon said. "Especially for somethin' I didn't even do."

He headed for the front door.

"Isaac!" Carlotta yelled.

When the front door opened, Cole Damon stepped out. Clint had hoped the man would go out the back door, try to get away.

"You Damon?" Sonnet asked.

"That's right. Who are you?"

"Jack Sonnet," Sonnet said. "You and your friends killed my brother."

"I never knew your brother, friend," Damon said.

"That ain't the word I got."

"Well, the word you got is wrong."

"Step down off that porch."

"I step down off this porch, I'm gonna have to kill you."

"You're welcome to try."

Cole Damon shook his head and came down the steps, stopped just at the bottom.

Clint was watching Damon and Sonnet when he saw a rifle barrel poke out one of the upper windows in the front of the house. He watched carefully, eventually saw the black face of the man holding the gun. Carlotta had put her man, Isaac, in the window to back Damon's play.

Clint shook his head.

Innocent bystanders.

Sonnet's move surprised Damon.

The man flinched as Sonnet drew, but that was the only move he had time to make. The bullet struck him in the chest and left him sprawled on his back on the steps, staring up at the sky.

On the second floor, Isaac watched as Sonnet gunned down Cole Damon.

"Oh Lord," he said to himself. "That Gunsmith fella was s'pposed to keep her young man alive. Miz Carlyle's gon' give him hell now."

He rose up, leaned out the window with his rifle.

Clint had no choice. As the black man sighted down the barrel at Sonnet, Clint drew and fired. Sonnet turned quickly, saw Clint, then looked up at the window as the black man fell to the ground.

Sonnet walked over to Damon's body to make sure he was dead.

Clint walked over to where the black man lay, found that he was very dead, too.

The front door opened and Carlotta stepped out, looked down at Damon, then glared at Clint and Sonnet.

"Damn you both to hell," she spat, then ducked back and closed the door.

Sheriff Atticus came to the scene, looked at the bodies, then stood off to one side with Clint.

"I tried to talk them both out of it," Clint explained. "They wouldn't have it."

"I suppose I'll have to go inside and talk to Carlotta. Of course, she'll claim you both murdered him and Isaac."

"Isaac gave me no choice," Clint said. "He tried to bush-whack Sonnet."

"And Sonnet?" Atticus asked. "He as fast as his grandpa?"

"Maybe faster."

"That'd be pretty damn fast. Why don't you take him to your hotel? I'll talk to both of you later."

"Sure. You figuring on an arrest?"

"I'm figurin' on you and your friend leavin' town in the mornin'," Atticus said. "That sound like a problem to you?"

"That doesn't sound like a problem to me at all, Sheriff," Clint said.

"Very good. Then I'll talk to you both later."

He went into the whorehouse.

SEVENTEEN

At the hotel they got Sonnet his own room, and Clint walked him there.

"Satisfied?" Clint asked.

"I told you I was satisfied even before I killed him," Sonnet said. "Why wouldn't I be satisfied now?"

"I meant with the room," Clint said.

"Oh," Sonnet said. "Yes, it's fine."

"I'll look in on you later," Clint said. "Maybe we'll get some supper."

"Yeah, okay."

Clint walked to the door.

"You're not mad at me?" Sonnet asked.

Clint stopped at the door and turned around.

"Why should I be mad at you?"

"Well, if you think I killed an innocent man—"

"Whether or not you killed an innocent man is your burden to bear, not mine, Jack," Clint said. "Besides, right now the only one of us we know for sure killed an innocent man is me."

He left.

* * *

"I've been thinking," Sonnet said later.

They were eating at Molly's, the small café that Sheriff Atticus claimed served a decent steak. Clint thought he was right. It was decent.

"About what?"

"About what you said."

Clint chewed his steak. Sonnet moved his around his plate.

"What did I say, Jack?"

"You know, about how maybe I was killing . . . an innocent man. This time."

"So," Clint said, "what are you thinking?"

"That maybe I should find out for sure who's guilty and who isn't."

"And if we find out that Damon was innocent?" Clint asked.

"I'll have to deal with that when the time comes," Sonnet said.

"Okay," Clint said. "Right now I suggest you finish your steak. It'll only be decent as long as it's hot."

Sonnet nodded, cut into it.

"Will you go with me?"

"To find out who killed your brother?" Clint asked. "Sure I will."

"I'm not sure I know where to start."

"That's because you're too used to having somebody tell you," Clint said. "We'll go back to where your brother was killed. We'll also try to track down where the telegrams have been coming from. Okay?"

"Okay."

They finished eating, then continued to talk over coffee.

"Haven't you wondered how he knows where to telegraph you?"

"No," Sonnet said. "I guess I was just happy that he was. So how does he do it?"

"I don't know," Clint said. "The only thing I can figure is that he's having you watched. Followed."

"Have you noticed anyone following us?"

"No."

"Then how—"

"That's just something else we'll have to learn later."

"When can we start?"

"Tomorrow."

"Do you think the sheriff will let us leave tomorrow?" Sonnet asked.

"Jack," Clint said, "I think he'll insist on it."

They were finishing up when Sheriff Atticus walked in and joined them.

"What'd you think?" the old man asked.

"You were right," Clint said. "The steak was . . . decent."

"Yeah, well," Atticus said, "it's the best in town." He waved to the waiter. "Coffee, Bill."

"Comin' up, Sheriff."

The waiter brought a second pot to the table, and all fresh cups.

"Steak, Sheriff?"

"Yeah, Bill."

"Comin' up."

As the waiter walked away, Clint poured the three of them some coffee.

"How did it go in the house?" he asked the old sheriff.

"Just like I said," Atticus answered, "Carlotta demanded I arrest the two of you for murderin' her two men."

"What'd you tell her?"

"That it was a fair fight," he answered. "Except for Isaac, that is. I told her that she's the one got him killed."

"She probably didn't take that well."

"She didn't. But that ain't gonna stop you fellas from leavin' town in the mornin'."

Clint looked at Sonnet, who nodded.

"If we're going to get an early start, we'd better get to our hotel and turn in, Sheriff," Clint said. "You don't need company while you eat, do you?"

"Naw," Atticus said, "I hate company while I eat. I hate talkin' while I eat."

Clint stood up, and Sonnet followed.

"Then we'll just say good night," Clint said, "and good-bye."

Atticus drank his coffee and waved as Clint and Sonnet went out the door.

EIGHTEEN

MONROE CITY, COLORADO

"What was your brother doing here?" Clint asked as they rode in.

"Meeting me."

"That's it?" Clint asked. "No business."

"Not that I know of."

"When did you find out he'd been shot?"

"When I got here."

"After you recovered from being bushwhacked?"

"Right."

"Where did that happen?"

"About fifty miles from here."

"And where did you recover?"

"At a farmhouse," Sonnet said. "Some people found me and took me in. They nursed me back to health."

"And who told you about what happened to your brother?"

"The local sheriff."

"Okay," Clint said, "we'll check in with him after we get a hotel room."

"And a real steak?"

"And a real steak."

Deputy Will Romer entered the sheriff's office, slamming the door behind him.

"Will, damn it," Sheriff Jubal Koster said, "how many times I gotta tell you not to slam that door?"

"Sorry, Sheriff, but I got news."

"Yeah, what news?"

"Two guys rode into town."

"That's news?"

"It's who they are that's news," the deputy said.

Koster, age forty and the sheriff of Monroe City for five years, looked at his young deputy.

"So who are they?"

"One of them is Jack Sonnet. You remember, that kid whose brother—"

"I remember," Clint said. "Who's the other one?"

"Clint Adams."

Koster frowned.

"What the hell is the Gunsmith doin' in Monroe City with Jack Sonnet?"

"Want me to go ask 'im?" Romer asked.

"No, Will, I don't want you to go and ask him," Koster said. "My guess is Mr. Adams will be comin' to see me."

"About what?"

"I guess we'll find that out when he gets here."

"You want me to watch him and Sonnet?"

"No," Koster said, "I want you to make your rounds and stay away from both of them."

"But—"

"You understand me?"

"Yeah, Sheriff," Will Romer said, "I understand."

"Now get out," Koster said.

"Okay, Sheriff."

Koster waited for his deputy to leave, then stood up, put on his hat, and left the office himself.

"This is a lot better than the steak we had in Deline," Jack Sonnet said.

"It sure is," Clint agreed.

There were also a lot more vegetables on the plate, and the coffee was better.

"We gonna see the sheriff today?"

"No, we'll make him wait until tomorrow."

"Make him wait?"

"If he's any kind of lawman, I'm sure he knows by now that we're here."

"Then shouldn't we see him right away?"

Clint shook his head.

"I want to give him time to think."

"About what?" Sonnet asked.

"His story."

"Are you sayin' he lied about my brother? About how he was killed?"

"We'll ask him about it," Clint said. "See if his story is the same as what he told you."

"Okay."

"Then I want to take a ride to that farmhouse where they nursed you back to health."

"What do you think they can tell you?"

"Do you have any idea who bushwhacked you?"

"No," Sonnet said. "I was gonna look into it after . . . after I finished with the men who killed Carl."

"Well, we're going to see if we can find it all out, Jack," Clint said.

"I really appreciate your help, Clint," Sonnet said. "My pa and my grandpa, they would, too."

"That's okay, kid," Clint said. "That's okay."

NINETEEN

Sheriff Koster entered the Silver Queen Saloon, stopped at the bar.

"Is Mr. Albert in?"

"He's in his office, Sheriff."

"Thanks."

The sheriff started walking away from the bar, but the bartender stopped him.

"You can't go in there unless I announce you," the man said.

"So announce me, then," Koster said. "But give me a beer first."

The bartender put a sloppily drawn beer on the bar for the sheriff, then walked to the back of the busy saloon.

"Come," a voice said when he knocked.

He stuck his head in the door and looked at Michael Albert, who was standing at a filing cabinet, reading some papers.

"What?"

"The sheriff's here to see you."

Albert looked at the bartender over his shoulder.

"What does he want?"

"He didn't say."

"All right," Albert said. He put the file back in and slammed the drawer closed. "Send him back."

"Right." The bartender returned to the bar, where the sheriff was nursing his beer.

"He says to go back."

"Thanks."

Koster slammed the beer mug down on the bar and walked to the back. He knocked and entered.

"Have a seat, Sheriff," Albert said.

Koster sat down across the desk from Albert.

"What's on your mind?"

"That Sonnet kid rode back into town today," Koster said.

"I thought we dealt with that," Koster said, frowning. "What does he want?"

"I don't know."

"You intend to find out?"

"If you say so."

"I say so," Albert said. "I want to know why the hell he's back here."

"Okay," Koster said, "I'll ask him."

When the sheriff didn't move, Albert asked, "Is there something else?"

"Uh, well, he's got another man with him."

"So?"

"It's Clint Adams."

Albert stared at Koster for a few moments.

"The Gunsmith?"

"That's right."

"You couldn't lead with that?" Albert asked. "I mean,

the news here is that the Sonnet kid rode back into town with the Gunsmith, right?"

"Well, yeah, I guess . . ."

"You guess?" Albert put his head back and stared at the ceiling for a few moments.

"You still want me to ask Sonnet what he's doin' here?"

"You better wait," Albert said. "If they're here for trouble, they'll come to you."

"That's what I told my deputy."

"Is it?" Albert asked. "Well, you must be getting smarter in your old age, huh, Sheriff?"

"Mr. Albert—"

"Just get out," Albert said. "Keep an eye on them and let me know when they come to you. Or if they do not come to you."

"Yeah, okay."

The sheriff stood up and left the office. The bartender watched him intently as he went out the batwings. Then he stole a look at his boss's door, which was closed.

Albert pushed his chair back from his desk, pressed his fingertips together in front of him, and stared at them. He should have had the Sonnet kid killed the last time he was here, but who thought he'd actually come back? And with the Gunsmith in tow? What was that all about?

Whatever was going on, he was sure that the sheriff wasn't going to be able to handle it.

He stood up and walked to the door of his office. He stood there until the bartender sensed him and turned to look, then he waved the man over.

"Yeah, boss?"

"Find me Benny Nickles."

"Nickles?"

"That's right."

"Bad news, boss?" the man asked.

"It is for somebody, Andy," Michael Albert said. "It is for somebody."

TWENTY

On the way back to their hotel, Jack Sonnet took Clint to the spot where his brother had died. It was a street outside Toth's Feed & Grain, across the street from the livery stable.

"Where was he going?" Clint asked. "Or coming from?"

"I don't know," Sonnet said. "All I was told was that he was shot right here. Apparently, five men braced him and shot him down on the street."

"And—if your information has been correct—three of those men are dead."

"Yes," Sonnet said, "if my information has been right."

Clint looked around, studied the buildings.

"Somebody could have seen this happen," he said. "Somebody outside the feed and grain, or the livery."

"The sheriff told me he checked for witnesses and didn't find any."

"Then how did he know five men shot and killed your brother?"

"I don't know."

"Somebody told him that," Clint said, "and that somebody was a witness."

"Seems like that should be right."

"Well," Clint said, "that's one of the questions we're going to ask the sheriff tomorrow."

"So what do we do tonight?"

"While we're here," Clint said, "let's talk to people at these two businesses."

"You want to split up?"

"No," Clint said, "I want to stay together. After what happened to your brother, I want everything we do in this town to be done together. Agreed?"

"Agreed."

They started with the feed and grain, talking to a man named Emmett Toth who claimed he never saw a thing. There were two other employees in the building, and they made the same claim. They didn't see—or hear—anything.

Clint and Sonnet left the building.

"How could five men shoot your brother down in the street, and yet nobody even heard a shot?"

"They're lying," Sonnet said.

"Hell yes, they're lying," Clint said, "but before we call anyone a liar to their face, let's go and see who was in the livery when it happened."

They entered the livery, found a kid about sixteen or seventeen mucking out stalls with a pitchfork. This was not the same livery where they had left their horses when they'd ridden in earlier. That one was in another part of town.

"Help you fellas?" the kid asked. "I don't see no horses with ya."

"We just want to ask you a few questions," Clint said.

The boy stuck his pitchfork in the ground and leaned on it.

"What's it about?"

"A few months ago a man was shot down right outside your door," Clint said. "You remember that?"

"Sure do," the kid said. "I ain't ever seen nothin' like that happen before."

"So you saw it?" Sonnet asked.

"Uh, no, I didn't," he said. "I mean, I ain't never been around when somethin' like that happened."

"So you weren't here when it happened?" Clint asked.

"I was workin' here," the kid said, "but I was in the back. In the corral."

"So you didn't see anything."

"Nossir."

"And you didn't hear shots?"

"Oh, nossir."

"But you said you were outside," Sonnet said.

"I was, but I was out back."

Clint decided to let that go for the moment.

"What about your boss?"

"What about 'im?"

"Was he here that day?"

"Um, I think he was around here . . . somewhere," the kid said.

"What's your name, son?" Clint asked.

"Eddie."

"Eddie, this fellow here is Jack Sonnet. It was his brother who was killed."

"Aw, gee," Eddie said. "I'm sure sorry."

"We really need to find witnesses to the shooting," Clint said.

"Are you a lawman?" Eddie asked.

"No," Clint said, "I'm just a friend. My name is Clint Adams."

The boy took a step backward.

"For real?" he asked. "The Gunsmith?"

"That's right."

"Oh, gee . . ."

"You got something you want to tell me now, Eddie?" Clint asked.

"I, uh, no . . ." Eddie said, but he couldn't look Clint in the eyes. "What, uh, what would you do if you found out who done it?"

"I'll kill anybody who killed my brother," Sonnet said. "What would you do, Eddie?"

"Um, the same, I guess."

"Look, Eddie," Clint said, "we're going to be in town for a while. We're staying at the Merchant Hotel. If you think of anything—or remember anything—let us know, will you?"

"I sure will, Mr. Adams," Eddie said. "I mean, I'd like to help, I really would."

"That's good, Eddie," Clint said. "That's really good, because we'd be willing to pay for the right kind of help."

"Pay?" the boy asked.

Clint nodded and said, "Pay."

TWENTY-ONE

They went back to their hotel, figuring they were done for the night.

"Tomorrow we'll start with the sheriff," Clint said. "See what he's got to say for himself."

"You think he'll remember?"

"A lawman doesn't forget that kind of shooting in his town," Clint said. "He'll remember it, and he'll remember you. What I'm interested in is whether or not his story is the same."

"Well," Sonnet said, "I remember every word he told me."

"I knew you would," Clint said. "You don't forget when somebody tells you someone you loved died."

"You've lost love ones?" Sonnet asked.

"Not family members," Clint said, "but lots and lots of friends."

They stopped in the saloon for a beer before going to their own rooms.

"What about somebody watchin' us?" Sonnet asked.

"I still haven't seen anybody," Clint said. "On the other hand, you haven't gotten a telegram since Deline, have you?"

"No."

"Then whoever was sending them must know that you've changed your plans."

"How?"

Clint shook his head, then thought of something.

"Jack, you haven't been keeping in touch with anyone, have you? Sending telegrams yourself?"

Sonnet didn't answer right away.

"Jack . . ."

"Just Betty."

"Who's Betty?"

"She's the daughter of the farmer who took me in," he said. "She's the one nursed me back to health."

"Oh yeah?" Clint smiled.

"We got . . . you know, friendly."

"And you've been sending her telegrams?"

"Just to tell her where I am," he said, "and that I'm all right."

Clint stood there and studied what was left of his beer.

"You don't think she'd tell anybody, do you?" Jack asked.

"I don't know the girl, Jack," Clint said. "But she wouldn't have to tell anybody."

"What do you mean?"

"Somebody could just be watching her, reading her telegrams."

"You mean . . . like her father?"

"Father, brother—"

"She doesn't have any brothers."

"Uncles?"

"There's an uncle."

"Okay, so maybe the father, maybe an uncle, maybe

somebody in town. We'll find out when we get there. Meanwhile, don't send any more telegrams."

"What? You mean . . . to Betty?"

"That's what I mean," Clint said. "Have you sent one yet from here?"

"Uh, no," Sonnet said. "I haven't had the time."

"Okay, don't," Clint said.

"But . . . she'll worry."

"After we talk to the sheriff," Clint said, "we'll take a ride out to that farm and see Betty and her family."

"The Rayfields."

"Okay," Clint said, "we'll go and see the Rayfields."

"Yeah, okay," Sonnet said. "I'm gonna turn in."

"I'll see you in the morning. We'll have breakfast right here in the hotel."

"Sure."

Sonnet left the saloon and went to his room, and Clint ordered a second beer . . .

He was halfway through the second beer when a man wearing a badge entered, not from the hotel lobby but from the street. He was young, obviously a deputy.

"Hey, Will," the bartender greeted him. "Does the sheriff know you're here?"

"I've gotta do my rounds, don't I?" the deputy said. "Let me have a beer."

"I'll give you a short one, just to keep you out of trouble."

Clint noticed that the deputy was having a hard time keeping his eyes off him, so he assumed the young man knew who he was. That probably meant the sheriff knew he was in town, and probably Jack Sonnet, too.

But the deputy was trying his best to ignore him.

TWENTY-TWO

Clint nursed his beer while the deputy talked with the bartender, waiting to see if the badge toter would finally give in and talk to him. But as much the young man was straining to, he was apparently able to resist the urge.

"I gotta get back to my rounds," the deputy told the bartender.

"Yeah, you better get out there."

The deputy gave one last sidelong look at Clint and then left.

"He's pretty young to be a deputy, isn't he?" Clint asked.

"Will? Yeah, he's a local kid the sheriff gave a job to."

"He seemed real interested in me, didn't he?"

"Oh, you noticed that?" the bartender asked. "I guess you know when you get recognized, huh?"

"It's kind of hard not to notice," Clint said. "What was his problem? He have orders not to bother me?"

"My guess is the sheriff wants to talk to you first," the bartender said. "Will has a habit of sayin' the wrong thing."

"I see."

"You want another one, Mr. Adams?"

"No," Clint said, pushing the empty mug away. "I think I'm going to turn in."

"You have a good night."

"Before I go," Clint said.

"Yeah?"

"There was a shooting in town a few months ago."

"Was that a friend of yours?"

"Didn't know him," Clint said. "But I heard about it. What can you tell me?"

"Not much," the man said, leaning on the bar. "Five men gunned down one. Nobody saw it."

"Nobody?" Clint asked. "That kind of a shooting and not one witness?"

The bartender shrugged.

"Or is it just that nobody is coming forward?"

"Don't know why that would be," the bartender said. "The man who was killed was a stranger. Nobody knew him."

"That does sound odd," Clint said. "What's your name?"

"I'm Dan."

"Thanks for talking to me, Dan."

"Sure, Mr. Adams," Dan the bartender said. "You have yourself a good night."

"You, too."

Clint left the saloon.

Outside, Will Romer crossed the street to where Sheriff Koster stood.

"Well?"

"He was in there."

"Alone?"

"Yup."

"Did you talk to him?"

"No, sir," Romer said. "I did what you told me."

"Okay," Koster said. "Now go home."

"But, Sheriff—"

"Go on home, Will," Koster said. "I'll see you in the morning."

"Yes, sir."

Koster watched his deputy walk away, then turned his attention to the hotel. He watched for about half an hour before he turned and also went home.

TWENTY-THREE

In the morning Clint waited for Sonnet in the lobby and then they went into the hotel dining room for breakfast. Over steak and eggs, Clint told Sonnet what his plan was.

"I want you to keep quiet," he said.

"What?"

"Let me do all the talking," Clint said, "unless I ask you a question."

"Well . . . okay."

"The sheriff is going to be curious about my part in this," Clint said. "He'll also be curious about why you're back here. We're not necessarily going to satisfy his curiosity in either case. But we'll see if we can get some of our own questions answered."

"Okay," Sonnet said. "I'll let you call the play, Clint."

They finished their breakfast, left the hotel, and walked over to the sheriff's office.

As Clint and Sonnet entered the sheriff's office, the man with the badge turned to face them.

"I was wonderin' when you two would show up," the man said. He had a coffeepot in his hand, finished pouring himself a cup, then walked to his desk without offering them any.

"Good morning, Sheriff," Clint said.

"Mr. Adams," Koster said. "What's the Gunsmith doin' in Monroe City?"

"You remember my friend, don't you?"

"Mr. Sonnet?" Koster said. "Sure I do. Jack, isn't it?"

Sonnet didn't answer.

"I guess I'm gonna be doin' my talkin' to you, Mr. Adams," Koster said. "My name's Jubal Koster."

"Obviously you know who I am," Clint said.

"Well, a man with your reputation can't ride into a town without being recognized."

"Probably not."

"What can I do for you?" Koster asked. "If you're here with young Mr. Sonnet, I guess this is about the murder of his brother."

"You want to tell me about it?"

"What's to tell?" Koster asked. "Somebody gunned down his brother. Nobody knows who."

"Somebody knows."

"If they do, they didn't tell me."

"How many shooters were there?"

"Five."

"Now see," Clint said, "if there were no witnesses, how do you know there were five shooters?"

"Well . . . yeah, somebody saw that there were five men, but nobody actually saw who they were."

"Okay, then," Clint said. "There you go. There's a witness. We'd like to talk to the witness."

"Why?"

"Because Mr. Sonnet here is interested in who killed his brother."

"I thought he knew," Koster said. "I thought he had the names and was trackin' them down."

"Well, somebody gave him some names," Clint said, "but we decided to try and find out for ourselves before killing anybody."

"I can't help you," Koster said.

"Can't? Or won't?"

"I'd like to," Koster said. "Really I would. But I can't."

"Why not?"

"The fella who saw the five shooters was a stranger," Koster said. "He's gone."

"What was his name?"

"Smith," Koster said, "John Smith."

"That's the name he gave you?" Clint asked. "Or the name you're giving me?"

"That's the name he gave me."

"And you believed him?"

"It didn't matter," Koster said. "He couldn't identify any of the men."

"Somebody was able to identify them," Clint said. "Somebody started sending Jack here one name at a time in telegrams."

"Then it sounds to me like he had all the help he needed."

"Not quite," Clint said, "because now there's some question about whether or not he was being given the right names."

"Oh, I see," Koster said. "Somebody gave him the names and he started killin'. Now he's wonderin' if he killed the right men."

"That's it."

"Well, I can't help you," Koster said.

"That may be true," Clint said.

"What do you mean, may?" Koster asked. "Are you callin' me a liar?"

"No," Clint said, "not yet anyway. When I do, you'll know. We'll talk again soon."

Clint turned and headed for the door.

"So, you don't talk anymore?" Koster asked Sonnet.

"I'll talk," Sonnet said, "when I have something to say."

Sonnet followed Clint out the door.

Outside, the young man asked Clint, "What did we accomplish there?"

"Koster now knows you're not just going to accept any answer," Clint said. "You want the right answer. And if I'm right, the sheriff is going to have to check with somebody on his next move."

"So what's our next move?"

"Like I said at breakfast," Clint said, "you're going to take me and introduce me to the Rayfields."

TWENTY-FOUR

The Rayfield farm was fifty-four miles east of Monroe City. Clint decided that he and Sonnet should camp along the way, so as not to startle the family by knocking on their door too late at night.

"After all," Clint said, "they're farmers. They'll be up early, and so will we."

They built a campfire a few miles from the farmhouse, prepared some beans and coffee.

"What's the next town?" Clint asked.

"Just a few miles beyond the farm is a small town called Garfield."

"Do they have a telegraph key there?"

"I know what you're thinking," Sonnet said. "I never got to go to that town, but that's where I been sending telegrams for Betty."

"So she hasn't been riding into Monroe City to pick them up."

"I don't think her father would let her do that."

"Okay," Clint said. "After we talk with Betty and her father, we'll take a ride to Garfield."

"Also her mother."

"What?"

"Her mother and her uncle, they'll be there, too."

"We'll talk to the whole family," Clint said.

"What makes you think they know somethin' they didn't tell me?" Sonnet asked.

"I don't know," Clint said. "Maybe they saw something when they found you that they don't know was important."

"Well," Sonnet said, "I don't remember anything until I woke up in their house."

"What happened before that?"

"I was just riding," Sonnet said.

"To Monroe City?"

"That's right."

"From where?"

Sonnet hesitated. Clint stared at his confused face across the fire.

"Don't you remember?"

Frowning, Sonnet said, "I guess maybe I don't."

"But you know you weren't coming from Garfield."

"I don't think I was ever in Garfield."

"And you didn't stop at the farm."

"No, I had never seen them before."

"You had to be coming from somewhere."

"There are a lot of little towns hereabouts," Sonnet said. "It could have been any one of them."

"All right," Clint said, "we'll let that go for now. But that may be something the Rayfields can help us with. Maybe you said something while you were unconscious."

"I guess."

"More beans?"

* * *

They decided to stand a watch, just in case somebody was following them—somebody so good at it that Clint couldn't tell.

Clint took the first watch, putting on another pot of coffee for himself.

Sonnet rolled himself up in his bedroll and fell asleep. He did not, however, sleep well. He rolled about fitfully, obviously having dreams that were not restful.

Clint didn't blame him. First his brother was killed. Then he started hunting down and killing men who might turn out to be innocent.

With that on his mind, Clint doubted he'd be able to sleep soundly either.

TWENTY-FIVE

In the morning they finished the beans and coffee for breakfast, and mounted up. Sonnet took the lead and headed for the farm.

"You didn't sleep very well last night, Jack," Clint said.

"I didn't?"

"You were tossing and turning," Clint said. "What were you dreaming about?"

"I don't know," Sonnet said. "I never remember my dreams."

"I suppose that could be a good thing," Clint said. "I always remember my dreams. Especially the bad ones."

"If you say I didn't sleep well," Sonnet said, "I guess that explains why I'm so tired."

"Don't worry," Clint said. "When this is over, you can sleep for a week."

"Maybe more," Sonnet said.

"Sure," Clint said, "maybe more."

As they approached the house, the sun was just starting to come up. They could see a man walking toward the house, shoulders already slumped, and smoke tendrils coming from the chimney.

As they approached, the man stopped walking and turned to face them.

"Good morning, Mr. Rayfield," Jack Sonnet said. "Remember me?"

"I remember," the farmer said, but he didn't look happy about it. "Yer just in time for breakfast. Put your horses in the barn."

"Thank you kindly," Sonnet said.

The farmer grunted and went inside the house.

Clint and Sonnet rode to the barn, dismounted, and walked their horses inside.

"He doesn't look too happy to see you," Clint said.

"I don't think Mr. Rayfield is happy about the way Betty and I feel about each other."

"You're talking like a man in love, Jack."

Sonnet ducked his head, but not before Clint saw his face color.

They took their horses to the barn, left them saddled, and gave them a little hay before walking to the house.

As they approached the house, the door opened and a woman stepped out, carrying a bucket of water.

"You can both wash up in here," she said.

"Hello, Mrs. Rayfield," Sonnet said.

"Hello, Jack," she said, and went back inside.

"Wow," Clint said, "also not very happy to see you."

"She's all right."

They rolled up their sleeves, washed up, and then went into the house.

"Jack!" a young girl said happily.

"Keep to your chores, girl!" Rayfield ordered from his seat at the table. "Get these men some coffee."

"Yes, Pa."

"Have a seat," Rayfield told them.

They sat at the table, across from Rayfield and another man who looked enough like the farmer to be his brother.

Betty came over and poured them some coffee.

"Thanks, Betty," Sonnet said.

She smiled and went back to the stove.

"Introduce your friend, Jack," Rayfield said.

"Mr. Rayfield, this is my friend, Clint Adams," Sonnet said.

"Clint Adams," the farmer said. "You bringin' trouble to my door, boy?"

"Papa!" his wife scolded. "These are our guests."

"It's all right, ma'am," Clint said. "He's got a right to ask. It seems to me, Mr. Rayfield, that you brought trouble to your door when you took Jack in a few months ago when he was injured."

Rayfield picked up a butter knife and pointed it at Clint.

"That wasn't my idea," the farmer said. "That was these foolish women."

The foolish women brought plates to the table that were piled high with eggs, ham, and biscuits.

"We couldn't very well leave him lying out there bleeding the way he was," the farmer's wife said.

"Still . . ." was all the farmer offered. He used his knife to spear a piece of ham.

"Papa, we have guests!" his wife scolded again. "Please, gentlemen, help yourselves."

"Thank you, ma'am," Sonnet said. "It all sure looks good."

The ladies took their seats and breakfast commenced. Everyone was either too hungry, or too nervous, to talk during the meal.

TWENTY-SIX

After breakfast Rayfield said, "Ben and me gotta get back to work."

Ben was the uncle that Sonnet had told Clint about. The man seemed very quiet, apparently did whatever his brother told him to do.

"Get your hat, Ben!" Rayfield snapped.

Ben Rayfield stood up, grabbed his hat, and followed his brother out the door, still chewing on a piece of ham.

"Mr. Rayfield doesn't seem very happy to see us," Clint said.

"Papa is just a sourpuss," Betty said.

"Betty!" Mrs. Rayfield said. "Clear the table."

"Yes, ma'am."

"What brings you back here with your friend, Jack?" the older woman asked. She and her husband were probably in their fifties, but hard work had aged them beyond those years.

Betty, on the other hand, was very young and pretty, and Clint could see why Sonnet was smitten.

"Ma'am, we're concerned about the men who tried to kill

Jack those months ago. Jack doesn't remember much about what happened."

"We didn't see anything, Mr. Adams," she said. "We only found Jack after the fact."

"Did he say anything?"

"About what?"

"Who might have shot him," Clint said. "Where he was coming from?"

"He didn't say anything that I heard," she said, "but it was Betty who was nursing him most of the time. Betty?"

"Yes, Mama?"

"Come here, girl."

The farmer's daughter came over to the table. She appeared to Clint to be eighteen or so, very blond and very healthy looking. She stood at least five-eight and was very solidly built.

"While poor Jack was unconscious, did he say anything?" Mrs. Rayfield asked.

"Well," she said, "he was mutterin' some, but I couldn't rightly understand everythin' he was sayin'."

"Did you understand any of it?" Clint asked. "Maybe the name of a man, or a town?"

"Well . . . he mentioned Busby once."

"Busby," Clint said. "What is that? A man?"

"Busby is a town about ten miles west of here," Mrs. Rayfield said.

Clint looked at Sonnet.

"You remember being in Busby?"

"No," he said, "not at all."

"I guess we'll have to take a ride over there and find out."

"When will you be leaving?" Mrs. Rayfield asked.

"Probably in a few minutes," Clint said. "There's no reason for us to stay around here and get in the way."

"Jack . . ." Betty said a bit reproachfully.

"Do you mind if we go for a walk?" Sonnet asked Mrs. Rayfield.

"Not if you don't keep her from her work," she said. "And stay away from her father. He'll just snap at you."

"Yes, ma'am."

Sonnet stood up, and he and Betty went out the door quickly.

Clint had an idea what they were in a rush to do, and he sincerely hoped they wouldn't run into her father while they were doing it . . .

"What has that poor boy been up to since he left us?" the woman asked.

"Ma'am, I think somebody might have been using him, taking advantage of his thirst for revenge and sending him after the wrong men."

"Innocent men?" she asked.

"Well . . . not exactly innocent, but possibly innocent of killing his brother."

"And has he already killed?"

"He has."

"That is a shame," she said. "He has all the makings of a fine young man."

"I agree, he does."

"But now he is a killer."

"Well, I wouldn't—"

She stood up and said, "Once you leave here, you will please make sure he never comes back."

"I don't know if I can do that, ma'am."

"If you do not," she said, "he and my husband will come to blows, and the result with be tragic."

Clint hesitated, then said, "I can see that."

"Then please," she said, "I ask for your help."

"I'll see what I can do."

Jack and Betty walked hand in hand until they were far enough away from the house, and nowhere near her father. They sank to the ground together, kissing, their hands groping. He unbuttoned her dress and peeled it down her arms so that her bountiful breasts sprang free. He held them in his hands, kissed them until the nipples grew hard, then nibbled on them until she moaned and cried. She massaged him through his trousers, then undid his buttons and stuck her hand inside.

They had done this a few times before he left, but had never gone so far as to consummate their love. This time there was no stopping them. He lifted her dress, touched her with his fingers until she was very wet. Then she slid his trousers down, lay on her back, spread her legs, and took him into her. There was a moment's resistance, and then she was a virgin no more. She cried out in pain first . . .

"Do you want me to stop?" he asked.

"No, no," she said into his ear, "never, never stop."

And he didn't. He moved into her slowly at first, then increased the tempo until he was ramming his cock into her.

Over and over. Her breathing came in gasps as she tightened her legs around him, raked his back with his nails, and exhorted him on . . .

Later, as they dressed hastily, she said, "You have to take me with you, Jack."

"I can't, Betty," he said. "Clint and I . . . we have killin' to do. You can't be around that."

"But I love you. You can't leave me here."

He took her by the elbows and said, "I'll be back for you, Betty. I swear I will."

He pulled her to him and she held on to him tightly.

"My father would kill you if he knew . . ."

"When I come back for you, Betty, we're gonna get married," he said. "I'll do it right. I'll ask your father for your hand."

"And if he refuses?"

He held her at arm's length and said, "Then we'll get married anyway. Nothing is gonna stop us. I love you, Betty."

"I love you, too, Jack."

By the time they walked back to the house, Clint had the horses ready.

"Oh!" Betty said, grabbing Jack's arm.

"I told you," he said, "I'll be back. I promise."

Betty walked to the house and went inside.

Sonnet joined Clint by the horses, accepted the reins of his mount.

"Did you say good-bye?"

"I did."

"Good."

"I also told her I'd be back."

"Maybe that wasn't so good."

"You can't stop me, Clint."

"Who said I was going to try, kid?"

They mounted their horses, started riding away from the house.

"Busby?" Sonnet asked.

Clint nodded and said, "First. Then we'll try Garfield."

They rode away in silence. No sense in trying to talk Sonnet out of returning—not now anyway, Clint thought. Not when the kid had that puppy dog look in his eyes.

TWENTY-SEVEN

Busby was a collection of falling-down shacks that could only be called a town through great generosity.

"Look familiar?" Clint asked.

"As a matter of fact," Sonnet said, "it does."

They reined in their horses in front of the trading post. When they entered, they saw that it was a combination general store and saloon. There was one man behind the bar, and three more in front, drinking. They all turned to look at the two strangers as they entered.

"You got a lot of nerve," the bartender said.

"Are you talking to me?" Clint asked.

"I'm talkin' to your friend," the man said.

"You didn't learn your lesson last time?" one of the other men asked Sonnet.

"My lesson?"

"Don't act like you don't understand," the bartender said. "When we kicked you outta town, we tol' you never to come back."

"I—I don't remember," Sonnet said.

"Can I ask a question?" Clint said.

"What?" the bartender asked.

"What gives you the right to kick anyone out of town?"

The bartender laughed, moved his vest aside to reveal a badge underneath.

"I'm the sheriff," he said. "I got the right to do anything I want."

"The sheriff."

"That's right."

"Of this . . . town."

"It ain't much," the man said, "but it's ours."

"And what did my friend do to get kicked out?" Clint asked.

"He knows."

"That's just it," Clint said. "He doesn't. Apparently, after he left, he got bushwhacked. Took him a while to recover, and he seems to have lost some of his memory."

"That's too bad," one of the other men said.

The sheriff and the three customers were all cut from the same cloth—dirty, unwashed rags. He didn't know what smelled worse, them or their clothes. They all looked to be in their thirties.

"Who are you?" Clint asked.

"Just a citizen."

"And you helped kick my friend out?"

"Oh, yeah."

The other two men laughed.

"And you?" Clint asked one of them.

"Just a citizen."

"And you?" Clint asked the third. "You just a citizen, too?"

"That's right," the man said around a chaw, "and we citizens like to help out whenever we can."

"Okay," the sheriff said, "you fellas have to leave now."

"We just got here," Clint said.

The sheriff pointed at Sonnet.

"He has to leave now," he said, "and since you're with him, so do you."

"I have some questions first."

"No questions," the sheriff said. He reached under the bar.

"Friend," Clint said, "if you come up from there with a shotgun, there's going to be a big mess to clean up here."

The sheriff hesitated just for a moment. Clint could tell from the look on his face he was going to make a terrible mistake. Then the man yelled, *"Boys!"* and went for the shotgun.

Clint drew and shot the "sheriff" right through the flimsy bar. He turned his attention to the "citizens," shot one of them as he was grabbing for his gun.

Sonnet was right there with him. He drew and fired twice, taking care of the other two citizens.

And then it was quiet.

"Look outside," Clint said.

Sonnet went to the door, peered out, and said, "Nobody."

"Could these be the only citizens in this town?" Clint asked. "And what the hell was that all about?"

"I don't know."

Clint reloaded as he checked the bodies. They were all dead. The "sheriff" had an old Greener shotgun behind the bar.

"Do you think he really was the sheriff?" Sonnet asked.

"I don't know," Clint said. "That star on his chest is kind of tarnished."

They stepped outside.

"Look around," Clint said. "Do you remember anything at all?"

"Like I said when we rode in," Sonnet answered, "it looks familiar."

"And those four inside?" Clint asked. "They look familiar?"

"No."

"They could be the ones who bushwhacked you," Clint said. "Apparently, they kicked you out of town, but that wasn't good enough. They rode after you and tried to kill you."

"But why?"

"I guess we won't find that out," Clint said. "Unless there's something—or someone—around here that can help."

"Let's take a look in these other buildings, then," Sonnet said.

"Okay," Clint said, "I'll take this one and the one next to it. You take the other two. Sing out if you find another citizen."

"Okay."

Clint turned around and went back inside while Sonnet walked across the street.

TWENTY-EIGHT

Clint went through the trading post front and back and found nothing. He stepped over the bodies as he was leaving. He didn't feel any responsibility to bury them. They'd made their own decisions.

The next building was smaller, and managed to look lived in and abandoned at the same time. He went through it and found nothing.

As he stepped outside, he saw Sonnet crossing back to him.

"Anything?" he asked.

"No," Sonnet said.

"I didn't find any records, any town charter," Clint said. "I doubt we killed an actual lawman here today."

"I'm glad to hear that," Sonnet said. "So, what do we do now?"

"Head for Garfield," Clint said. "If that's a legitimate town, there's probably a sheriff we can talk to about what happened here."

"Turn ourselves in?"

"Report what happened," Clint said. "That's a little different. You want to get a drink before we go?"

"No," Sonnet said. "I don't want to go back in there."

"No," Clint said, "neither do I. Let's just go."

They mounted up and rode out of Busby.

It only took a few hours to reach Garfield, which may have been smaller than Monroe City but certainly qualified as a town. There were people on the streets, several saloons, a couple of hotels, and—to Clint's satisfaction—a telegraph office. He realized at that moment that they had never asked Betty where she'd been receiving her telegrams. Sonnet would have known if he had only asked while he was sending one, but apparently it never mattered to him.

"There," Clint said, pointing at the sheriff's office.

"Right now?" Sonnet asked.

"No time like the present," Clint said. "I'd like to get it over with."

"Okay," Sonnet said. "I'll follow your lead."

They were about to enter the sheriff's office when the door opened and a man stepped out. He stopped short and stared at them. Clint saw the shiny badge on his chest.

"Sheriff," he said. "We were just coming to see you."

"Well," the man said, "you don't wanna go in there. It's a mess." He was a short, rotund man in his forties, who used a pudgy hand to wipe his mouth. "Can we talk in, say, the saloon?"

"Sure," Clint said, "why not?"

"Then come across here with me, boys," the lawman said. "Saloon's right over here."

They followed the man across the street to a small saloon.

As they entered, several men called out to the sheriff, and he returned their greeting.

At the bar he said, "Jasper, I'll have a beer. Let these gents have what they want."

"And who's payin', Sheriff?" the barman asked.

"Well . . ."

"I am," Clint said.

"See?" the sheriff said. "Set 'em up. Three beers."

The bartender obeyed, and accepted the money from Clint.

The sheriff drank down half of his beer and then turned to Clint.

"What can I do for you boys?"

"Well, we just came from a town called Busby."

"Busby?" the lawman said. "That ain't no town. Nothin' but a collection of wood."

"Then there's no legal law there? A sheriff?" Clint asked.

"There's a fella there wears a rusty badge, uses it to try to fleece folks who ride by," the lawman said. "But he ain't no legal lawman."

"Well . . . I suppose that's good to hear," Clint said.

"Why's that?"

"Because I killed him."

"What?" The sheriff stopped with his glass halfway to his mouth.

"Actually," Sonnet said, "we killed him—him and three of his citizens."

"Wait a minute," the sheriff said. "You killed all four of 'em?"

"They didn't leave us much choice," Clint said. "No choice at all."

"You mean somebody finally stood up to those fuckers?" he asked, laughing. "Well, that's great."

"You, uh, might want to send some men out there to bury them."

"No need for that," the sheriff said. "No need at all. I'm sure that'll be taken care of."

"By varmints," Sonnet said.

"Most likely," the lawman agreed. "You fellas want another?"

"No, thanks," Clint said. "We've got some . . . other things to do." He was going to say they had some "eating" to do, but he was afraid the sheriff might try to invite himself along.

"Well, all right, then," the sheriff said. "Enjoy your time in our town."

"Don't you even want to know who we are?" Clint asked. "After we killed four men?"

"Naw, I don't need to know that," the man said. "Just like you fellas don't need to know my name. Now, off with you. Enjoy your time in Garfield. Oh, and try not to kill anybody."

Clint looked at the sheriff, who was hard at work trying to wheedle a free beer out of the bartender, then turned and said to Sonnet, "Come on."

TWENTY-NINE

"That's a lawman?" Sonnet asked.

"Not much of one, obviously," Clint said, "but at least we won't have any trouble because of Busby."

"So now what?"

"Let's go to the telegraph office and ask a few questions."

"You ask," Sonnet said. "Like I said, I'll follow your lead."

Clint nodded, and led the way.

When they reached the telegraph office, they had to wait for the clerk to finish with another customer before he turned his attention to them.

"What can I do for you gents?" the tall, middle-aged man asked.

"Do you know the Rayfield family?" Clint asked.

"Sure do," he said. "They've got a farm outside of town. Right pretty young daughter, too."

"Betty," Sonnet said.

"That's right."

"Tell me something," Clint said. "For a while she was coming in here receiving telegrams, wasn't she?"

"Well, yeah, she was."

"Do you know where the telegrams came from?"

"All different places."

"But who from?"

"The same fella each time."

"What fellow?" Clint asked.

"I don't remember his name."

"Jack Sonnet?"

The man brightened.

"Yeah, that was it. Sonnet."

"That's me," Sonnet said.

"You're the lad?" he asked.

"That's right."

"Then why you askin'—"

"I want to know," Clint said, "who else saw those telegrams."

"Well . . . no one," the clerk said. "I ain't allowed to show 'em to anybody else."

"You could get fired, right?" Clint asked.

"That's right."

"Well," Clint said, taking some money from his pocket, "we're not going to tell anyone, are we, Jack?"

"No, we ain't," Sonnet said.

"Watch the door, will you, Jack?"

"Gotcha."

Sonnet went to the door.

"I—I can't tell ya nothin'," the clerk said.

"Well, there are two ways we can do this," Clint said. "You can tell me what I want to know and I'll give you some money."

"Or?"

"Or," Clint said, "we can do it the hard way."

"The hard way?"

Clint nodded.

"W-What's the hard way?" the clerk asked.

"You don't really want to know," Clint said. He held up the money. "You choose."

He slapped Jack Sonnet on the back and said, "Let's go."

"He told you?"

"He told me."

They stepped outside.

"He gave you a name?"

"He did," Clint said. "Tell me, have you ever heard of a man named Benny Nickles?"

THIRTY

They rode back into Monroe City several days later.

"They're back," Deputy Will Romer told Sheriff Koster.

"I knew they'd be back."

"What are you gonna do now?" the deputy asked.

Koster already had his feet up on his desk, so he just folded his hands in his lap and said, "I'm gonna wait."

"For what?"

"Never mind," Koster said. "Just make your rounds."

"Make my rounds, make my rounds," Romer complained. "You're always tellin' me to make my rounds."

"That's because it's your job!" Koster shouted after him as he went out.

"Where to first?" Sonnet asked as they rode in.

"Hotel," Clint said.

"Then what?"

"Steak?"

"You always eat steak."

"Not always," Clint said. "Just most of the time."

"Are we gonna go lookin' for this fella Benny Nickles?" Sonnet asked. "I mean, the clerk did say he lived here, didn't he?"

"He said he picked up the telegrams and brought them here."

"I don't get that part," Sonnet said. "Why pick up the telegrams? Why not just have them sent on to the telegraph office here?"

"Maybe they didn't want anyone else involved," Clint said. "We just have to find this Benny Nickles and find out who hired him to pick up your telegrams."

"And do what with them?"

"Keep track of you," Clint said. "Send you telegrams. Have you kill people for them."

"But why?"

"We'll find that out," Clint said. "This time we won't leave Monroe City without some answers."

"But first a hotel," Sonnet said.

"And a livery stable for the horses," Clint said.

"You think the sheriff knows anything about this?" Sonnet asked.

"I suppose we'll have to ask him, won't we?"

Koster entered Michael Albert's office.

"What is it?"

"They're back," Koster said. "You said you wanted to know when they came back. Well, they're back."

"What are they doing?"

"They put their horses up in the livery, got a hotel room, and now they're eating."

"That's it?"

"That's it."

Albert thought a moment, then said, "All right."

"All right?"

"You can go," Albert said.

"What should I do?"

"Nothing," Albert said, "don't do a thing, Sheriff. And make sure the same goes for your deputy."

"All right."

Koster left, and Albert sat back in his chair to think. Now that Clint Adams and Jack Sonnet were back, they were going to have to be dealt with. And he thought he knew who could deal with them.

Benny Nickles.

THIRTY-ONE

"Chicken," Sonnet said to the waiter.

"And you, sir?" the waiter asked Clint.

"Steak."

"Comin' up."

"Does it seem to you like we're always eatin'?" Sonnet asked.

"Eating is one of the most important parts of the day," Clint said. "That and drinking coffee."

"Not your coffee."

"Hey," Clint said, "I make good coffee."

"We been ridin' together long enough for me to tell you, no, you don't."

"That's just a matter of opinion," Clint said, "and I'll thank you to keep your opinion to yourself."

"Clint Adams?" Benny Nickles said.

"That's right."

"And a member of the Sonnet family?"

"Right again."

Nickles stared at his sometime boss.

"Do you have a problem with this?" Albert asked.

"Not as long as you're willin' to pay," Nickles said.

"Oh, I'll pay," Albert said, "as long as you get the job done."

"So let me get this straight," Nickles said. "You want me to kill 'em?"

"I want you to kill them if it looks like they're going to get close to me," Albert corrected.

"And who decides that?"

"You can decide," Albert said. "I'll trust you to analyze the situation."

"What if I kill Adams just because I want to?" Nickles asked.

"That's up to you," Albert said, "but in that case, you don't get paid."

"Might be worth it anyway," Nickles said. "That man's got a big reputation."

"Like I said, up to you."

"The kid," Nickles said, "he's supposed to be pretty good, too, right? Like his pa and grandpa?"

"That's what I've heard."

Nickles, a handsome man in his mid-thirties, tapped his knees with his right index finger while he thought over the situation.

"You taking the job, Benny?"

"I'll need some money in advance."

Albert opened his top drawer, took out a brown envelope, and tossed it to Nickles's side of the desk.

"That do?" he asked.

Nickles picked it up, hefted it, then put it in his pocket without counting it.

"For now," he said.

Nickles stood up and walked to the door.

"So I guess this means the kid didn't get the whole job done, right?"

"That's right."

"Too bad."

"Well," Albert said, "that might leave more work for you later."

"One thing at a time, Mike," Nickles said, "one thing at a time."

THIRTY-TWO

Clint and Jack Sonnet sat in wooden chairs in front of their hotel.

"Let me guess," Sonnet said. "We're makin' the sheriff wait . . . again."

"Right."

"Or maybe somebody will try something."

"Right again."

"Wouldn't that be stupid?" Sonnet asked. "I mean, it's a big town. It's gonna be pretty hard for us to find out who was sending me those telegrams."

"Somebody wanted those men dead," Clint said. "That somebody is going to get nervous the longer we're in town."

"So you think that person will send someone after us?" Sonnet asked.

"That would be helpful."

"Do you think that's what happened to my brother?"

"I don't know, Jack," Clint said. "Did your brother have any kind of reputation?"

"Carl was not a fast draw," Sonnet said. "He didn't inherit that family trait."

"But he was still the son and grandson of men with reputations."

"That's right," Sonnet said, "but why should he have to pay for that?"

"That's the problem with reputations," Clint said. "They tend to hurt a lot of people."

"Have you had that problem?"

"More times than I care to count," Clint said.

"Is that why you have to be careful about what you pursue?"

"Yeah, but I didn't pursue it," Clint said. "It pursued me."

"Unlike me, you mean," Sonnet said. "You think I'm tryin' to build a reputation?"

"No," Clint said, "you're stuck with it. You're third generation. Instead of pursuing it, you're going to have to run from it."

"Maybe," Sonnet said, "but not yet. Not until I find the men who killed Carl."

"And we're back where we started," Clint said.

"You have a lot of patience," Sonnet observed.

"Patience keeps you from going off half-cocked, Jack," Clint said. "You just need to take the time to think before you act."

"Well, you're sure giving me a lot of time to do that."

"I'm giving someone else the time to think, too."

They sat there until late afternoon, and then Clint said, "Time to talk to the sheriff."

"You think he's got something to tell us?"

"I think he does," Clint said. "The question is, will he tell us?"

Clint got up and Sonnet followed. They walked to the sheriff's office and entered. Koster wasn't there, but Deputy Will Romer was.

"Hello, Deputy," Clint said.

"Uh . . ." the deputy said.

"Clint Adams."

"Uh, yeah, I know," Romer said. "And, uh, Jack Sonnet, right?"

"That's right," Sonnet said.

"Uh, the sheriff's not here right now," Romer said. "He should be back soon."

"That's okay," Clint said. "We can talk to you."

"About what?"

"About five men gunning down one. Where were you when that happened, Deputy?"

"Uh, I dunno."

"You know about the shooting, right?" Clint asked.

"Well, sure," Romer said. "Everybody in town knows about it."

"Were you a deputy then?"

"I was, yeah."

"So where were you when it happened?"

"I dunno," he said again. "Probably makin' my rounds."

"If you were here—right here in this office—would you have been able to hear the shots?"

"I dunno."

"Come on," Clint said, "five shooters. How many shots must that have been? Somebody had to have heard it. It must have sounded like a battle."

"I guess."

"Isn't that something that would bring most lawmen running?"

"Um, sure."

"So where was the sheriff?"

"I, uh . . ." He hesitated.

"Yeah, okay," Clint said. "You don't know. Is he off talking to his boss now?"

"He's probably with Mr. Alb—"

The door opened then and Sheriff Koster walked in. He stopped short when he saw them. The deputy stopped before he could say the name that was on his lips. So close, Clint thought.

"What's goin' on?" the sheriff asked.

"Nothing much," Clint said. "Your deputy was just helping us out with some information about the shooting."

"What the—"

"I didn't say nothin', Sheriff. I swear."

"Get out," Koster said. "Make your rounds."

"Yessir."

Romer hurried from the office. Koster moved around behind his desk.

"What did he tell you?" he demanded.

"Something about the noise," Clint said. "I mean, with that many men firing their guns, it must've sounded like the Battle of Bull Run."

"He didn't hear a thing," Koster said. "He wasn't even here."

"Here in town?" Clint asked. "Or here in the office?"

"Whatayou—"

"I mean, from here," Clint said, "I think you'd be able to hear the shots. One shot, maybe two might go unnoticed, but that many? Makes me wonder why half the town didn't come running, let alone the sheriff."

"I told you," Koster said, "I didn't hear a thing."

"Not sure I believe that, Sheriff," Clint said, "not sure at all."

THIRTY-THREE

"You're callin' me a liar?"

"Oh yeah," Clint said, "and so's my friend here. Only he's not as patient as I am. He won't wait for me to prove you're a liar."

"Really?" Koster asked. "So you're threatenin' me?"

"No threat," Sonnet said. "If I find out—no, if I think you had something to do with my brother's death, I'll kill you."

"A lawman?" Koster asked. "You'll kill a lawman?"

"I'll kill you," Sonnet said. "Whether or not you're wearin' a badge won't matter to me."

"That is," Clint said, "unless you want to tell us that somebody else was involved?"

"Like who?"

"I don't know," Clint said. "That's why I'm asking you."

"I think you fellas better get out of my office," Koster said.

"Sure, Sheriff," Clint said.

"But I'll be seein' you again," Sonnet said. "Soon."
They turned and went outside.

Outside, Clint said, "You caught on pretty quick."

"It seemed to me you wanted to press him," Sonnet said.

"I did," Clint said. "Let's see what he does now."

"You think he's workin' for someone here in town?" Sonnet said.

"Definitely," Clint said. "Somebody with money. Those
people always think they can buy the law."

"Must be quite a few people in town who match that
description."

"Mmm," Clint said. "We could look into that."

"How?"

"There are two kinds of people with that information,"
Clint said. "Bartenders, and newspapermen."

"I can check with the bartenders," Sonnet said.

"And I'll check the newspaper," Clint said. "I'll meet you
in the saloon in our hotel in about two hours."

"Fine," Sonnet said, "I'll hit that one last."

"See you then."

They separated from there.

THIRTY-FOUR

Clint found there was only one town newspaper, the *Monroe City Chronicle*. The office was about three blocks from the sheriff's office. As he stood out front, he thought it would have been pretty hard not to have heard those shots from here.

The name of the newspaper was etched on all the windows, and the glass was frosted, so he was unable to see inside. He tried the door, found it unlocked, and went inside.

It was quiet, the printing press sitting unattended. He looked around, didn't see anyone, but there was an inner office behind a frosted glass door, again with a name etched in the glass. This time, however, instead of the newspaper, it bore the name of the editor: J. ABBOTT, EDITOR-IN-CHIEF.

He knocked on that door before opening it and entering.

A woman turned and stared at him, her eyes wide.

"You startled me," she said.

"I'm sorry," he said. "I was looking for J. Abbott, the editor."

"That would be me," she said.

"You're J. Abbott?"

"Jennifer," she said.

Her honey-colored hair was piled high on top of her head. She was wearing a purple, high-collar blouse underneath a brown jacket, and a matching brown skirt and boots. She looked to be in her late thirties, maybe forty, but she was lovely nevertheless.

"And you are?"

"Oh, my name is Clint Adams."

"Clint . . . Adams?" she said. "You mean . . . the Gunsmith?"

"That's right."

"Well . . . wow," she said. "What is the Gunsmith doing in Monroe City?" She grabbed up a pad of paper. "And can I quote you?"

"Um, no, you can't quote me," Clint said. "I came here to ask some questions, not answer them."

"Well, you can understand if I'm more experienced asking them than answering them."

"I do understand," Clint said. "But my questions are very simple."

"Well," she said, "maybe we can come to an understanding."

Clint did know why he'd met so many attractive newspaperwomen in his life. Was there something about the job that made the women in it appealing?

"Miss Abbott, I just need to know who the rich men in town are."

"That's it?" she asked. "You could get that information from any bartender in town."

"I know that," he said, "but I thought while I was here, I'd have a look at your coverage of the shooting that took place a few months back."

"The shooting?"

"Five men shot down a man named Carl Sonnet."

"Of course. I know what shooting you're referring to."

"Well, nobody else in town seems to want to admit to knowing about it," Clint said. "At least, everybody claims to have heard and seen nothing."

"Well, it was a terrible thing."

"Tell me," Clint said, "were you able to hear the shooting from here?"

"Actually, I didn't hear anything that way."

"How could that be?" Clint asked. "That much shooting would have made plenty of noise."

"Well," she said, "the printing press . . ."

"I see," he said. "Can I look at a copy of your newspaper from the next day?"

"We are a weekly paper," she said, "but I can show you the issue that covered the shooting."

"I'd appreciate it."

"Come in the back with me," she said. "That's what we consider our morgue."

He followed her to a back door that led to a hallway, then along that hall to another door, which she opened with a key. The interior of the room smelled musty. She lit a lamp and he could see the stacks of newspapers on shelves.

"Wow," he said, "this is a lot of paper for a weekly."

"We started out as a daily," she said. "Feel free to look through it all."

"Thanks," Clint said. "Where's the most recent—" But before he could finish his question, she was gone, closing the door behind her.

He started leafing through papers . . .

When he came out, the printing press was still not running. He reentered the editor's office, and she turned to look at him from her desk.

"Find what you wanted?"

"I did."

"What did you learn?"

"That everybody in this town is probably deaf and blind," he said. "Thanks for the look."

He started for the door.

"Wait," she said.

"Yes?"

She walked to him and handed him a piece of paper.

"What's this?"

"The list you wanted," she said. "Richest men in town? I included some of the ranchers in the area."

"Oh . . . thanks."

"Didn't think I was going to come through, did you?" she asked.

"Well . . ."

"Look," she said, "I'd love to do an interview with you while you're in town, but that's up to you."

"I appreciate that."

"I do ask one thing."

"What's that?"

"If you come across anything that's newsworthy, you'll let me know?"

"Miss Abbott," he said, "since you're the only newspaper in town, you'll be the first to know."

THIRTY-FIVE

When Clint got to the saloon in his hotel, Sonnet was already there, nursing a beer.

"Beer," Clint said to the bartender.

The bartender set one up.

"What'd you get?" Sonnet asked.

Clint showed Sonnet the list.

"I got the same names," Sonnet said, "except for these two."

"Those are ranchers," Clint said.

"You got this from the newspaper?"

"From the lady editor herself."

"So we've got . . . what, seven names."

"Right."

"Seven men who might have the sheriff in their pocket?" Sonnet said. "Seven men who could have been sending me those telegrams."

"We could take them alphabetically," Clint said, "but I think we should check on the ones in town first. Save the ranchers for later."

"And how do we do that?" Sonnet asked. "I mean, how do we check them out?"

"Well," Clint said, "we could ask them."

"And they'll tell us the truth, right?" Sonnet asked sarcastically.

"First of all, you're too young to be that sarcastic," Clint said, "and two, yeah, they'll tell us the truth—at least, six of them will. That seventh one? He's not going to be too happy to see you."

"So where do we start?"

"Well, there's an Emmett Toth on this list."

"We already talked to him."

"Right," Clint said. "He's the one who owns the feed and grain. According to this list, he also owns several other businesses in town. Let's talk to him again."

Benny Nickles took a bill from the envelope Michael Albert had given him and handed it to Marcy Wilkes.

"Oooh," she said, "money." She grabbed it between her fingers, then rubbed it between her small breasts and over her already turgid nipples. She was a black-haired girl with very dark brown nipples, and accepted the fact that she was Benny's girl—that is, when he wanted her to be.

"Ha ha!" Nickles laughed. "And lots more where that came from."

He leaned forward, took one of her nipples between his teeth, and rolled it there.

Marcy dropped the money to the mattress and grabbed his head with both hands.

"I love it when you do that," she said.

She slid one hand beneath them and grabbed hold of his hard, jutting cock.

"Mmm," he growled deep in his throat, "and I love it when you do that."

"That?" she asked, sliding down between his legs. "Or this?" She swooped down on him with her mouth, taking him all the way inside, then bobbing up and down on him, gobbling him up.

"Oh," he said, putting one hand on her head, "definitely that."

Michael Albert was having much the same experience, except that the girl on her knees in front of him was not there by choice, and she wasn't being paid for her services. Actually, she was on salary as a saloon girl, but sucking her boss's cock was just something she had to do every once in a while to keep her job. All the girls there had to be willing to do it if they wanted to keep working there. And since he paid so well, none of them really complained about the extra duty—much.

"That's it," he said, guiding her head by putting one hand behind it, "nice and wet and slow."

Sex served two purposes for Albert. Sometimes, he was just mindless in his pursuit of pleasure for pleasure's sake. Other times—like this—going nice and slow helped him to relax, and to think.

That's what he was doing in that moment. He had his head back, and was letting his thoughts work themselves out. Clint Adams . . . Jack Sonnet . . . Benny Nickles . . . even Sheriff Koster, were all in there, being sorted out. Actually, having each one of those men dead would not have done anything to ruin his day. But it was better to take one thing at a time.

"Slower," he told the girl, Emmy, "slow down, I don't want to finish yet."

Emmy let his penis slide from her mouth, happy to do so. She took some deep breaths.

"In fact," he said, "hike that skirt up and come and sit on this thing for a little while. There's a good girl . . ."

THIRTY-SIX

"I ain't got nothin' to say to you two," Emmett Toth said. "I told you last time I didn't hear nothin'."

"That's true, Mr. Toth," Clint said, "you did tell us that. What I want to know is, why?"

"Huh? What's that?"

They were standing in the middle of his feed and grain, rather than in the privacy of his office. His other employees were watching.

"Well, sir," Clint said, "the shooting took place right outside this building. How could you not have heard anything?"

"I was busy," Toth said, "workin', and so was everybody else. You're gonna have to find your answers someplace else."

"Did you have something against my brother?" Sonnet asked. "Or my family?"

"What are you talkin' about?" Toth demanded. His eyes were red-rimmed beneath bushy white eyebrows, and his thick cracked lips and yellow teeth were surrounded by a huge, white beard. "I didn't even know your brother."

"But you know who the Sonnets are, don't you?" Clint asked.

"Huh? The Sonnets? Gunfightin' family, ain't they?" the man asked.

"That's their reputation, yeah," Clint said. "But Carl, he wasn't any kind of hand with a gun. Fact is, one man with a gun could have shot him down. There was no need for five to do it."

Toth's eyes became less angry, and a little wary.

"I wouldn't know nothin' about that."

Clint looked at Sonnet and nodded.

"Mr. Toth," the younger man said, "I've been huntin' down the men who killed my brother. Fact is, I been getting telegrams giving me their names, one at a time."

"That right?" Toth said. "Sounds like somebody's tryin' to help you, boy. You should be grateful."

"The only problem is," Clint said, "they may have been the wrong names."

"Which means," Sonnet said, "I may have killed the wrong men."

"Why come to me with this?" Toth asked.

"Because," Sonnet said, "if it turns out you were sending me those telegrams, there'll be hell to pay. And I'll be the devil's collector."

Sonnet turned and walked away.

Toth looked at Clint.

"You got something to say?" Clint asked.

Toth opened his mouth, but nothing came out. In the end, he shook his head. Clint turned and followed Sonnet outside.

After Clint Adams and Jack Sonnet left the feed and grain, Emmett Toth took his apron off and tossed it aside. The gesture was both angry and impatient.

"Willie!"

A young boy about seventeen came running over. He was also wearing an apron.

"I have to go out," he told the boy. "I'll be back shortly."

"Okay."

Toth started for the back of the building.

"Where are you goin'?" Willie called. "I thought you said you were—"

"I'm going out the back!" Emmett Toth snapped impatiently.

Willie watched his boss go with a confused frown on his face, then went back to work.

Benny Nickles put Marcy on her back, straddled her, and beat his hard penis on her belly. The sound of flesh smacking flesh filled the room.

"What are you doin'?" she asked.

"Teasin' you."

"Uh, why?" she asked. "You've never teased me before."

"I'm in a good mood," he said. He took the head of his penis and pressed it to her moist slit, slid it up and down, wetting her even more.

"Jesus," she said, "that feels good."

He stuck the head of his dick into her, then withdrew it.

"You bastard!" she said. "Stop teasin' me, or I won't be in a good mood."

"What do you want, then?" he asked with a smile.

"I want you to fuck me," she said, "hard!"

"You don't like the gentle Benny?" he asked.

"I hate the gentle Benny!"

He smiled and said, "Okay, then," and drove his hard cock into her.

She gasped and opened her legs wide . . .

*   *   *

Emmy bounced up and down on Michael Albert's lap until
he thought he had his thoughts organized. Then he grabbed
her beneath the arms and began bouncing her even harder.
She was a petite girl and was completely helpless in his
hands. Her head bounced around on her neck, and just as
she thought her neck would break, he exploded inside her.

In the next moment he literally lifted her off his cock and
tossed her aside. She landed painfully on her butt on the
floor.

"We're done," he said. "Go back to work!"

She got to her feet, straightened her dress, and left the
office. He closed his pants, turned his chair so that he was
facing his desk.

He needed to see Benny Nickles, because he had changed
his mind. He was tired of waiting . . .

"What do you think?" Sonnet asked.

"He may not be the one who sent the telegrams," Clint
said, "but I think he knows something. He went from angry
to worried pretty quickly."

"Then maybe we should go back in and press him," Sonnet suggested.

"We've got other people to talk to," Clint reminded him.
"And maybe one or more of them will know something, too.
By the time we're done, somebody may want to talk to us."

"You think one of these men will give another one up?"

"If only to keep himself in the clear," Clint said. "And it
may be more than one. I've always found that rich men will
work together almost as much as they'll compete with each
other."

"Have you known a lot of rich men?"

"Enough to know that I usually don't like them."

They started to walk away from the feed and grain building.

"I've got a question," Sonnet said. "If I killed the wrong men, then there are still five men out there who killed my brother."

"That makes sense."

"And they might still be here in town."

"Also makes sense."

"So what if they come for us?" Sonnet asked.

"I think they'll find we won't be as easy a target as your brother was," Clint said.

THIRTY-SEVEN

Clint and Sonnet talked to three more of Monroe City's wealthiest citizens. The banker, Thomas Benedict, seemed genuinely confused about why they would come to him. Clint decided he was not involved.

Louis Blake owned the general store, and two restaurants in town. He appeared nervous when they talked about the shooting, but then everybody did. When they talked about the telegrams sent to Jack Sonnet, he seemed baffled. Clint put him on the list with the banker.

And the third man was Benjamin Atwill, who was the mayor of Monroe City.

"I understand you've been talking to some of our prominent citizens," Atwill said after he admitted Clint and Sonnet to his office.

"How do you know that?" Clint asked.

Atwill, a large, pale-faced man in his sixties, laughed and said, "Because they all came running to me after you spoke with them, starting with Toth. You frightened the poor man out of his wits."

"The banker didn't seem very frightened," Clint said.

"Oh, Tom Benedict was just confused. He thinks the sheriff should run you both out of town."

"That might be harder than it sounds," Clint said.

"Well, all right," Atwill said, "you might as well give me the same treatment you gave them, and we'll see how frightened I become."

"After this, we still have a few other men to see," Clint said. "Will you be sending warnings to them?"

"Hell, no," Atwill said. "I'll let each of them deal with you themselves. Now, come on. What's this all about?"

"I think you know what it's about, Mayor," Clint said.

"The unfortunate shooting of Carl Sonnet."

"Yes," Jack said.

"Why does nobody in town admit to seeing or hearing anything?" Clint asked.

"I think you'll have to ask them that question," Atwill said.

"We have. Repeatedly. What about you?" Clint asked. "What did you hear?"

"From here?" the mayor asked. They were in the second floor of the brick City Hall building. "I heard a barrage of shots."

Clint and Sonnet exchanged a glance.

"You're the first one to admit that," Clint said.

"It sounded like a battle," Atwill said. "How could I lie and say I didn't hear it?"

"So what did you do?" Sonnet asked.

"I looked out my window." Mayor Atwill indicated the plate glass window behind him. "I can actually see much of the town from here."

"And could you see the scene of the shooting?" Clint asked.

"Unfortunately, no," the mayor said.

"So what did you do?" Sonnet asked.

"Nothing," Atwill said. "I'm a little out of shape and old to go running down there. Besides, that's not my job."

"So the sheriff ran down there," Clint said.

"It was his job," Atwill said.

"But he found no witnesses."

"That's what he said."

"And you believed him?"

"Why not? Why would he lie?"

"Did you expect him to make an arrest?" Clint asked.

"If possible."

"But he never did," Sonnet said.

"I suppose he wasn't able to catch them," Atwill said. "Or find out who they were."

Clint just stared at the mayor.

"So," the politician said, "what are your intentions, gentlemen?"

"I'm going to find the men who killed my brother," Sonnet said, "and I'm going to kill them. And it doesn't matter to me who they are."

"Meaning what?"

"Meaning," Clint said, "it could be a prominent citizen, it could be a sheriff, or . . . a mayor."

"Now that's a threat," Atwill said.

"No threat," Sonnet said, "just fact."

"Mr. Adams, you should caution your young friend, here—"

"I'm cautioning you, Mayor," Clint said. "Somebody sent Jack here after the wrong man at least once. We're not only going to find the right men, but we're going to find him, as well."

"You're going to force me to hire extra deputies," Atwill said. "Special deputies."

"Is that something you do a lot, Mayor?" Clint asked.
"Hire special deputies?"

"When there's a need."

"And how many do you usually hire?" Clint asked.
"Five?"

THIRTY-EIGHT

Outside City Hall, Clint said to Sonnet, "This town's a mess."

"I don't care," Sonnet said. "I'm not leaving here without finding my brother's killers, no matter what I have to do, or what we leave behind."

"I have a feeling we only need to talk to one more man," Clint said.

"Not the ranchers?"

"I think the man we're after is somebody in town," Clint said, "and I think the other prominent townspeople know who it is."

"Who's left?"

"Michael Albert," Clint said. "He owns the biggest saloon in town."

Sonnet was quiet.

"What are you thinking?" Clint asked.

"The biggest saloon in town," Sonnet said, "was something my brother never could have resisted."

"Then let's have a look," Clint said.

* * *

They entered the Silver Queen Saloon and went right to the bar. The place was packed, which explained why Michael Albert was one of the wealthiest men in town.

At the bar they ordered two beers and then Clint asked the bartender, "Where's your boss?"

"Mr. Albert?"

"He owns the place, right?" Clint asked.

"That's right."

"Then that's who I want to see."

"And who are you?"

"Clint Adams."

"Wait here."

The bartender left the bar and walked through the crowd to the back of the room. Clint and Sonnet took a look around, saw that several men were watching them.

"This feels good," Clint said.

"Meaning?"

"Meaning it feels bad," Clint said. "There's any number of men in here who could be part of the five."

Sonnet looked around more intently.

"Why don't they just come after us?" he asked. "That would make it so much easier."

"Looking at these people," Clint said, "I can see how nobody from here would have bothered to run down the street when they heard the shots."

The bartender returned, didn't get behind the bar, and said, "Follow me."

They followed the man through the crowd, some of whom turned to watch them go. Clint walked behind Sonnet, and kept an eye out for backshooters.

At a door the bartender knocked and opened it.

"Boss, the Gunsmith is here."

"Let him in."

Clint let Sonnet go in first. The man behind the desk looked tense, but was trying to look relaxed. Clint noticed that the top-right-hand drawer of his desk was ajar.

"That's all," Albert told the bartender.

The man left, closing the door.

"You're Adams?" Albert asked.

"That's right."

"And you?"

"Jack Sonnet."

"Ah," Albert said, "it was your brother who was shot here a few months ago."

"That's right."

"What brings you to me?" Albert asked.

"We've been talking to prominent citizens in town," Clint said, "about the shooting. They seem to feel you were behind it."

Sonnet looked surprised for a moment before he recovered.

Michael Albert smiled at Clint and said, "Nobody told you that."

"Well," Clint said, "let's say men like Toth, and the mayor, sort of intimated it. They said nobody else had a motive."

"And what would my motive be?"

"I don't know," Clint said. "Maybe you'd like to explain to this man why you had his brother killed."

"Mr. Sonnet," Albert said, "I did not have anything to do with your brother being killed."

"Well," Clint said, "somebody in town did. And somebody in town was sending telegrams to Jack here, giving him names of men who were supposed to have killed his brother."

"Not me," Albert said.

"Then who?" Clint asked.

"How would I know?"

"Look," Clint said, "it takes a lot of money to hire five men to kill somebody. I intend to find out which one of you prominent citizens did it."

"And when we find that out," Sonnet said, "I'm gonna kill him first, before I kill the others."

"You think you can just ride into town and starting killing people?" Albert asked.

"Yes, sir," Sonnet said. "I've already killed at least two of the men who murdered Carl. I'm planning to kill the rest, and one more—the man who hired them."

"And I'm going to back his play," Clint said.

"You know, there's law in this town," Albert said.

"We know that," Clint said, "and the mayor told us he'd hire special deputies if he thought he needed to."

"So I think the best thing for everyone would be if you two left town."

Clint and Sonnet had not sat down. Now Clint moved toward the door and said, "That's not going to happen, Mr. Albert. I suggest that you, or whoever's in charge, send those same men after us—the ones who are left—and then we'll see what happens."

"I'm a businessman, Mr. Adams," Albert said. "I don't employ gunmen."

"It has been my experience, Mr. Albert," Clint said, "that it's businessmen who *can* afford gunmen."

Clint noticed Albert's eyes going to his desk drawer. He was sure there was a gun in there. But a man who paid for guns would never have the courage to go for one himself.

"We'll talk again," Clint said. He let Sonnet go out ahead of him, and followed.

* * *

Another door opened and Benny Nickles stepped in.

"You heard?" Albert said.

"I did."

"It's time for you to do something."

"He doesn't know a thing," Nickles said. "He's bluffing."

"I want them dead."

"If we try this and we don't succeed, they'll know it was you."

"Then you better get the job done."

"I'll need some special deputies."

"I'll talk to the mayor," Albert said. "Get your men together."

"Usual paycheck?"

"More," Albert said. "You get this done and there'll be a lot more."

THIRTY-NINE

"Why did you push that hard?" Sonnet asked outside.

"Because," Clint said, "whether he's in this alone or with one or two of his colleagues, he's the one who has access to the men."

"How can you be sure?"

"I just didn't like him."

"Well," Sonnet said, "maybe we pushed hard enough that somebody is going to come after us."

"Special deputies," Clint said.

"Will that be a problem for you?"

"About as much of a problem as it was to kill the man with the badge in Busby. 'Special deputies' will just be another name for hired guns."

"So what do we do now?" Sonnet asked. "Just wait?"

"No," Clint said. "I say we push even harder."

"Who?" Sonnet asked.

"The man behind the real badge," Clint said. "I want to push him a little more and see what we can get."

"Now?"

Clint nodded and said, "Now."

Clint could tell by the look on Koster's face that the man wasn't happy to see them.

"What do you want now?"

"We've just come from talking to your boss," Clint said.

"I work for the town, Adams," Koster said. "If you want to say I have a boss, that would probably be the mayor."

"Oh, we talked to him, too," Clint said. "But I was talking about Michael Albert."

"Mr. Albert is a saloon owner," Koster said. "How would that make him my boss?"

"Money," Clint said. "It always comes down to money."

"Are you accusing me of taking payoffs?"

"I'm accusing you of being the worst kind of lawman, Koster," Clint said. "You're either crooked, or incompetent."

"You got a lot of nerve—"

"I think you're the one with the nerve, Sheriff," Sonnet said. "You got nerve wearin' that badge."

"Mr. Sonnet," Koster said. "I understand your grief over your brother's death—"

"Don't talk to me about my brother's death," Sonnet said. "You haven't done a thing about it since it happened. Well, Clint and me, we are doing something about it."

"You've got a choice, Sheriff," Clint said.

"What's that?"

"Change sides," Clint said. "Enforce the law with us, or stay where you are and go against us."

Koster studied the two men, and for a moment Clint thought he was going to say or do something useful.

"You're only two men," he said instead.

"It took five men to gun down my brother," Sonnet said.

"It'll take a lot more than that to gun down me and Clint Adams."

Sonnet turned and left.

"This ain't the way to go, Adams," Koster said.

"Then you tell me, Sheriff," Clint said. "Save us all a lot of trouble. Tell me what happened that day. Tell me who was sending Jack Sonnet all over the country to kill men who might have been innocent."

"Nobody's innocent," Koster said. "Everybody's guilty of something."

"Present company included, Sheriff," Clint said. "Present company included."

FORTY

Michael Albert looked at the half a dozen special deputy badges Mayor Atwill dropped on his desk.

"Pin 'em where you need 'em," Atwill said. "Just get the job done."

"I'll give them to Nickles," Albert said, picking them up.

Atwill pointed a finger at Albert from behind his desk.

"This better work," Atwill said. "You really messed things up when you had that Sonnet kid killed."

"Who knew he was part of that family?" Albert asked.

"Sonnet?" Atwill repeated. "That wasn't a clue for you?"

"Okay, look," Albert said, "I made a mistake with one Sonnet. I won't make a mistake with the other."

"Never mind Sonnet," the mayor said. "Don't make any mistakes with the goddamned Gunsmith!"

"Don't worry," Albert said. "This will get done."

"It better!"

Later, in his own office, Michael Albert laid the badges down on his desk.

"Six?" Nickles asked.

"You gonna need more?" Albert asked.

"Maybe," Nickles said. "This is the Gunsmith we're talkin' about."

"Well," Albert said, "hire as many as you need, but there's six badges."

Nickles picked one up and pinned it on, then scooped up the other five and put them in his pocket.

"Just let me know when it's over," Albert said.

"You'll know the same way you knew last time," Nickles said. "By the noise."

"And don't worry," Albert said. "Nobody'll come running. Not in this town."

"If that idiot sheriff shows up too soon again, I'll put a bullet in him, too," Nickles said.

"Suits me," Albert said.

Nickles nodded and walked out.

In a run-down saloon at the south end of town, Benny Nickles laid the five badges out on a table. Seven men—three from the last shoot-out and four new ones—were gathered around him.

"There's only five," Simon Dent said. "There's seven of us."

"First come, first served," Nickles said.

The men all grabbed for the badges. The two slowest stood back with frowns on their faces while the others pinned on their badges.

"So whatta we do?" one of them asked.

"Don't worry," Nickles said. "You're all special deputies."

"Gettin' paid the same?" asked the other of the men without a badge.

"Exactly the same," Nickles said.

"How do we do this, Benny?" Dent asked.

"Same way as last time," Nickles said. "Catch them out in the open."

"And when do we do it?"

"No time like the present," Nickles said.

"What about the law?" somebody asked. He wasn't one of the original five men who'd gunned Carl Sonnet down.

"It's just like last time, boys," Nickles said. "We are the law."

FORTY-ONE

Clint and Sonnet went into a small café and ordered coffee. For a change, they sat by the window. Clint wanted to be able to see the street.

"We just gonna sit here?" Sonnet asked.

"For a while," Clint said. "I want to see what kind of activity we might have caused."

Sonnet looked out the window.

"Look like folks going to and from work to me," he said. "Like always."

"Keep watching."

As they watched, there seemed to be fewer and fewer people on the street.

"What's happening?" Sonnet asked.

"The word's getting around," Clint said. "People are getting off the street."

"So they're coming?"

"They're coming."

"That means it was Albert," Sonnet said. "He had Carl killed."

"Or he went to the mayor, who told him what to do. Or one of the others."

"What if it's one of the ranchers we haven't talked to?"

"Then we'll find out," Clint said. "When they come for us, we have to make sure we take at least one alive."

"So we have to be careful *not* to kill them all?" Sonnet said. "Couldn't we get killed doing that?"

"It's possible," Clint said, "but we're going to need somebody to tell us who hired them."

"I thought we knew it was Albert."

"Albert, or the mayor, or one of the others," Clint said. "We still can't be sure."

Sonnet finished his coffee.

"You want to be sure, don't you, Jack?" Clint asked. "Before you kill someone else?"

"I didn't," Sonnet said. "I didn't care before, but yeah, you've made me care. So yeah, I want to be sure."

"Okay, then."

Clint poured them both more coffee.

"What was the name of that fella?" Sonnet asked.

"Which one?"

"The one the clerk in Garfield told us about."

"Oh. Benny Nickles."

"Maybe he's the one coming," Sonnet said.

"Could be."

"Maybe we should have asked around town about him."

"You're probably right," Clint said. "We can go and ask a bartender or two about him. But how about some pie first?"

"Benny Nickles?" the bartender said. "Sure, I know him."

"How well?" Clint asked.

"Well enough not to answer questions about him."

"He's that kind of man?" Clint asked.

"Yeah," the bartender said, "that kind."

"Hard man?"

"The hardest."

They were in a small saloon called The Buffalo Chip. Not the most attractive name for a place, but Clint wanted to ask his questions in a small saloon, not a large one.

"He ever come in here?" Clint asked.

"I tol' you," the bartender said, "I don't answer questions that could get me killed."

"So he's a killer," Clint said. "For hire?"

The man didn't answer. He was a small man, with small hands and features. His features looked worried now.

"Like a special deputy?" Clint asked.

"Mister . . ."

"Yeah, okay," Clint said. "Okay. Thanks for your help."

Outside, Sonnet said, "His help?"

"What he said without saying it."

"So now we know Benny Nickles is not just an errand boy, he's a killer."

"Right."

"So let's find him."

"Let's let him find us, Jack," Clint said.

"But maybe we'll find him alone," Sonnet said. "If he finds us, he'll have some men with him."

"I know."

"You think you and I can go up against five, six men?" Sonnet asked. "And live?"

"I've seen you use a gun, Jack," Clint said. "Don't worry about it."

"Where?"

"Where what?"

"Where should we wait for them?"

Clint thought a moment, then said, "I think I know the perfect place."

FORTY-TWO

Nickles had four men out scouting the town, looking for Clint Adams and Jack Sonnet. It was Dent who spotted them and went to the saloon to tell Nickles.

"I got 'em," Dent said.

"Where?"

"You ain't gonna believe it."

Nickles stared at him and said, "Try me."

After Dent told him, he said, "Find the others. It's time."

"Here?" Jack Sonnet asked Clint. "Right here?"

"Right here," Clint said.

Sonnet looked around at the livery, and the feed and grain, then down at the ground where his brother had been found.

"But why?"

"Because," Clint said, "they won't be able to resist."

"You think?"

Clint nodded, said, "I think."

"So we . . . what?" Jack Sonnet asked. "Just stand here?"

"No," Clint said, "we stand here . . . and wait."

Dent said, "Should we surround 'em? Come in from the other side?"

"No," Nickles said.

"Why not?"

They stopped walking when they came within sight of the street in front of the feed and grain.

"Look at 'em, Dent," Nickles said. "They're waitin' for us."

"Why are they doin' that, Benny?" one of the others asked.

"Maybe," Nickles said, "they just got a hankerin' to die."

"You sure we got enough guns, Benny?" Dent asked. "I mean, I ain't got a hankerin' to die."

"Hey," Nickles said, "five of us were enough to take care of one Sonnet. I think eight of us can kill a Sonnet and the Gunsmith."

Nickles turned to look at his "deputies."

"I'm keyin' on the Gunsmith," he said. "I'll make the first move, and then the rest of you start shootin'."

"You think you can take Adams?" Dent asked.

"I think I'm gonna try," Nickles said.

"W-What if he kills you?"

"We can't all live forever," Nickles said.

Dent knew Benny Nickles was crazy. The man had no fear of death.

"Start walkin'," Nickles said.

"Here they come," Clint said.

The special deputies came walking up the street toward them. Clint looked around. There was nobody watching from the feed and grain, or from the livery. And there was nobody on the street.

"This is the perfect place in town to kill somebody," Clint said. "Nobody can see anything, and nobody will come running to see what happened."

"That's real comforting," Sonnet said. "There's eight of 'em, Clint."

"Well," Clint said, "at least three of them killed your brother, Jack. And that big one in front? Got to be Benny Nickles. I'll take him."

"Why?"

"I'm going to try to keep him alive."

Sonnet sighed and said, "Okay."

The eight men were getting closer.

"Shouldn't we have more guns?" Sonnet asked.

"You got six bullets?" Clint asked.

"Well, yeah."

"Me, too," Clint said. "That should be plenty."

"What if we miss?"

Clint looked at Sonnet and said, "Don't."

FORTY-THREE

Sheriff Koster sat at his desk, waiting for the noise. It was probably going to sound even louder and longer than the last time. And this time, he was going to have to wait longer before he showed up.

"Sheriff?" Will Romer said.

"Yeah?"

"Should I make my rounds?"

"Just sit tight, Will," Koster said. "Just sit tight."

Mayor Atwill stood at his plate glass window, looking down at his town. He'd seen Benny Nickles and the other deputies walking down the street, so he knew they were moments away from getting the job done. He listened intently for the shots.

Michael Albert sat behind his desk. Business was brisk in his saloon, and the racket would keep him from hearing the shots.

If this didn't work, he would lose everything.

He opened his top drawer and looked at the .32 Colt he kept there.

"How close do we let them get?" Sonnet asked.

"Not much closer," Clint said. "Remember, try not to hit the big guy in front. I think that's Nickles."

"Yeah, yeah," Sonnet said. "Jesus, what would my grandpa think if he knew I was drawing my gun and trying *not* to kill somebody?"

"I'm sure, in this instance, he'd forgive you."

"Aw, crap," Sonnet said as the group of men started to draw.

As they closed in on the two men, Benny Nickles grinned, kept his eyes on Clint Adams, and drew his gun, knowing his men would follow.

What a reputation he'd have after this!

Clint drew quickly. Even a man with his skill knew better than to try any trick shots in this kind of situation. Grandpa Sonnet was right—when you drew your gun, you shot to kill.

But Clint fired his first shot very carefully, watched as his bullet struck the big man—Nickles—in the right hip. He knew that bone shattered as the man went down . . . and then lead was ripping through the air . . .

Jack Sonnet fired twice, each shot striking home. Then he dropped to one knee as a couple of bullets whizzed over his head. After that everything seemed to be happening in slow motion, but that's what his grandpa told him it meant to be a Sonnet. In this kind of situation, you saw everything . . .

* * *

Clint fired again as the special deputies opened up—those who were still standing. Sonnet had already put two down, and Clint had done the same. With Benny Nickles on the ground, that left three deputies standing.

Two of them turned to flee. Clint might have let them go, but Jack Sonnet had other ideas. He didn't know which of these men had actually killed his brother, so he just figured to kill them all.

The final man was in a complete state of panic. He didn't know whether to fire at Clint or at Sonnet, but the decision was made for him when they both shot him . . .

Koster thought the barrage of shots had ended too quickly.

Way too quickly.

"Sheriff?" Will asked. "Are we goin'?"

"In a minute."

The mayor heard the shots, felt like the job was being done properly, until the shots suddenly stopped.

Too soon.

Way too soon.

Michael Albert's office door opened and the bartender stuck his head in.

"Boss?"

"Yeah?"

"It's over."

"Over?" Albert asked. "W-When did it start?"

"A few minutes ago."

"And it's over already?'

"Yessir."

Albert covered his eyes with his left hand.

"Okay," he said. "Get out."

As the door closed, he reached for the .32 with his right hand.

Clint and Sonnet walked among the bodies, found them all dead—except for the big man. They reloaded as they went along.

"Jesus!" the man screamed. "This hurts!"

"Are you Benny?" Clint asked.

"Yeah," Nickles said. "Get me a doctor. Why'd you shoot me in the hip?"

"I wanted to keep you alive."

"Christ," Nickles said, squeezing his eyes shut, "I think I'd rather be dead."

"That can be arranged," Sonnet said, drawing his gun again.

"No, no, wait!" Benny said, extending his hands.

"You want a doctor?" Clint asked.

"Yeah, I do!"

"Then you got some talking to do," Clint said.

FORTY-FOUR

Clint and Sonnet entered City Hall with some onlookers watching them.

"Seems like folks don't have a problem coming out to see what's happening in this part of town," Clint said.

They went up the stairs to the second floor. The door to the mayor's office was closed. They went in without knocking.

"Jesus," Mayor Atwill said, "stop him, will you?"

Standing in front of the man's desk, pointing a gun at him, was Michael Albert.

"Get out, Adams."

"Can't do that, Albert," Clint said. "We've got business with the two of you. See, Benny Nickles told us you were the one sending Jack those telegrams, sending him after those men."

"Yeah, that's because Mayor Atwill here told me to. It's all his fault." He risked a look over his shoulder at Sonnet. "Hey, kid, he's the one had your brother killed."

"That's a lie!" Atwill said. "He did that, sent Nickles and those others after your brother."

"Because he told me to!" Albert said. "He's the one you wanna kill. I've been holding him here for you."

"Why?" Sonnet asked.

"What?" Albert asked.

"Why was my brother killed?"

"He found out that the mayor has been looting this town since he took office," Albert said. "Little by little."

"Yes, but with his help," the mayor said.

"He's the one in charge."

"So you both had Carl Sonnet killed," Clint said, "and you just tried to have us killed."

"He told me to send those special deputies after you," Albert said.

"Special deputies were his idea," Atwill said.

"What about the men I killed?" Sonnet asked. "Kennedy, Williams, Damon—did they shoot my brother down, or were you just using me to get rid of your enemies?"

"Relax, kid," Albert said. "Kennedy and Williams were guilty as sin. Those two were in the shoot-out that killed your brother. You and your friend here just finished off the other three. Damon, well, he was the mayor's partner in raiding the town coffers, until he ran off—"

"With your portion of the take," the mayor finished for him.

"You mean yours," Albert said. "So you see, kid—"

"I'm not a kid," Sonnet grumbled, but he was relieved that he hadn't murdered any truly innocent men.

"What's going on?"

Clint turned, saw Sheriff Koster standing in the doorway with his deputy.

"Sheriff, you're just in time," Clint said.

"For what?"

"Like I said before," Clint said, "to pick sides. We have a witness who will testify that these two men sent eight men to kill us, just as they sent five men to kill Carl Sonnet."

"Mayor?" Koster asked.

"Arrest him, you idiot!" Atwill said, pointing at Michael Albert.

"Albert," Clint said, "put the gun down. You know you're not going to use it. You don't have the nerve."

"I—I wasn't going to kill him," Albert said. "I was just h-holding him."

Clint stepped forward and plucked the gun from Albert's hand.

"Sheriff," Clint said, "would you like to arrest these men and hold them for the federal marshal?"

"Federal marshal?" Koster asked.

"Yes," Clint said, "along with Benny Nickles, after the doctor finishes patching him up."

"Benny?"

"Clint," Sonnet said, "wait—"

"Jack," Clint said. "It's over. Let the federal marshals take it from here."

Sonnet looked at the mayor, and at Albert, both of whom appeared very frightened.

"Jack?"

"Yes," Sonnet said, "yes, all right, Clint. I suppose it's over. The five men who killed my brother are dead."

Clint slapped him on the back.

"Sheriff?" Clint said. "You've been looking the other way. Now's the time to do the right thing."

Koster ran his hand over his face.

"Sheriff?" the deputy asked.

"Yeah, Will," Koster said, "yeah, put them under arrest."

"Yes!" Deputy Romer said, looking at Clint. "This is *much* better than making my rounds."

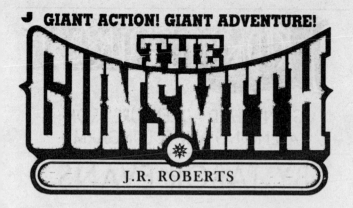

GIANT ACTION! GIANT ADVENTURE!

THE GUNSMITH

J.R. ROBERTS

LONGARM

GIANT-SIZED ADVENTURE FROM AVENGING ANGEL LONGARM.

BY TABOR EVANS

2006 Giant Edition:

LONGARM AND THE OUTLAW EMPRESS

2007 Giant Edition:

LONGARM AND THE GOLDEN EAGLE SHOOT-OUT

2008 Giant Edition:

LONGARM AND THE VALLEY OF SKULLS

2009 Giant Edition:

LONGARM AND THE LONE STAR TRACKDOWN

2010 Giant Edition:

LONGARM AND THE RAILROAD WAR

2013 Giant Edition:

LONGARM AND THE AMBUSH AT HOLY DEFIANCE

penguin.com/actionwesterns

M456AS0812

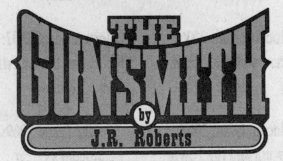
M11G0610